RECKLESS MOTORCYCLE CLUB OPEY TEXAS

wicked

RECKLESS MC OPEY TEXAS CHAPTER

WALL STREET JOURNAL & USA TODAY BESTSELLING AUTHOR

KB WINTERS

Copyright and Disclaimer

This book is a work of fiction. The names, characters, places and incidents are products of the writer's imagination and have been used fictitiously and are not to be construed as real. Any resemblance to persons, living or dead, actual events, locales or organizations is entirely coincidental.

Copyright © 2019 Book Boyfriends Publishing

All rights reserved. No part of this publication may be reproduced, stored in or introduced into a retrieval system, or transmitted, in any form, or by any means (electronic, mechanical, photocopying, recording, or otherwise) without the prior written permission of the copyright owner. The author acknowledges the trademarked status and trademark owners of various products referenced in this work of fiction, which have been used without permission. The publication/use of the trademarks is not authorized, associated with, or sponsored by the trademark owners.

Table of Contents

Copyright and Disclaimer ii

Chapter One 7

Chapter Two 21

Chapter Three 33

Chapter Four 45

Chapter Five 61

Chapter Six 81

Chapter Seven 87

Chapter Eight 95

Chapter Nine 101

Chapter Ten 111

Chapter Eleven 121

Chapter Twelve 125

Chapter Thirteen 139

Chapter Fourteen 155

Chapter Fifteen 165

Chapter Sixteen 187

Chapter Seventeen 205

Chapter Eighteen 229

Chapter Nineteen 235

Chapter Twenty 259

Chapter Twenty-One 269

Chapter Twenty-Two 293

Chapter Twenty-Three 309

Chapter Twenty-Four 319

Chapter Twenty-Five 329

Chapter Twenty-Six 339

Chapter Twenty-Seven 351

Chapter Twenty-Eight 355

Chapter Twenty-Nine 367

Chapter Thirty 375

WICKED

Reckless MC Opey Texas Chapter Book 2

By Wall Street Journal & USA Today Bestselling Author

KB Winters

Chapter One

Saint

Gunnar strolled into the bunkhouse and held up the Tulip Gazette, looking like somebody put a bug up his ass.

"Have you guys seen this shit?" he said, scowling at us and acting all pissed off again. The guy had it made in the shade. I rolled my eyes. What now?

"Chili cook-off?" Cruz, the new Road Captain, guessed with a snicker.

"Rummage sale?" Slayer, the new club Treasurer, added but only because of the glare Gunnar sent Cruz.

"No, assholes," Gunnar sneered. "Some fucker's robbed the downtown business district at gunpoint again." Gunnar paused, waiting for anger or outrage or some kind of reaction. I rarely could tell what Gunnar expected outside of The Barn Door.

I laughed at the idea that anything in Opey was a 'district' much less a business district. "You mean that piece of land where the courthouse, post office and a few other shops come together?"

"Yeah, I do," he growled. "It's six blocks of businesses that sustain this town, including Hardtail Ranch and The Barn Door. Nearly thirty-five businesses exist down there. This is the third armed robbery in as many weeks."

The room fell silent again.

Apparently, I wasn't the only one in the bunkhouse who didn't know what Gunnar wanted.

"No offense man, but how in the hell is this our business?"

Leave it up to Wheeler to say what the rest of us were thinking. Maybe that was what made him a solid choice for club VP.

"This is our business because it is literally our fucking business," he shot back at the VP with fire in his eyes. "First of all, armed robbery means there's a crew operating around here and we don't know who it is. That's a problem."

"Why? We're not even criminals so what difference does it make?" None of it made sense to me, why in the fuck did we need to give a damn about a band of criminals? "I mean, it's shitty for the businesses that got hit, but how is this a Reckless Bastards problem?" The room fell silent, either because I'd voiced what everyone was thinking or, more likely, I'd stepped in the shit. Again.

Gunnar let out a deep, cleansing breath and raked a hand through his hair that seemed to go from 'just out of the military' short to desperately in need of a haircut. "No, Saint, we're not criminals, but we're the only ones who know that. What do you think the good folks of Opey think of us, no matter how they smile and chat with us in town?"

Slayer barked out a laugh. "Old Debbie Gallagher at the diner swears I'm up to no good and that's just because of the long hair." He punctuated his words by running his fingers through said brown locks.

"That's just how it goes, but that means we have to be extra diligent about what the fuck goes on in Opey. Any hint of a serious crime and we'll be the first suspects." I opened my mouth to object but Gunnar stopped me with an ice cold look. "Most of us are new to town which is already a strike against us in this small ass town, but the fact that we also are Harley enthusiasts is bound to make us a target."

"Then are we doing it? The club's official?" At first this whole motorcycle club thing sounded good, even fun. But over the past few weeks Gunnar had been trying to make it a big damn *thing* and I wasn't sure how I felt about that. "Seriously."

"Riding's in my blood, man. This is how it goes. You knew that when you agreed to join. Right?" Wheeler had his back up, shoulders squared so he was at his full six feet four inches of intimidating asshole.

"Well I didn't realize we'd be targeted as criminals or be responsible for cleaning the town of the criminal underclass!" It was an unusual outburst from me, even I knew that, but this was too much. First, it was just a club, a brotherhood of men with similar backgrounds in search of a place to heal and grow after the military. Then it was shared financial interest, which in all fairness, had been a spectacular perk. Now it was vigilante justice or...some stupid shit like that.

"Is that a problem, Saint?" The way Gunnar said my name, like he was my cold, distant stepfather pissed me off. Made me wonder why the fuck any of this sounded like a good idea to me.

"Hell Gunnar, I don't know. This is the first I'm hearing of this." My gaze bounced around the room at the other so-called brothers and of all the expressions I saw, none resembled anything like understanding or solidarity. Mostly blank looks and a few confused ones. "Am I the only one confused about this?"

Holden lifted a hefty, plaid-covered arm in the air. "I must admit Gunnar, I'm a bit confused about this, too. What are you suggesting we do here?"

A moment of uncertainty flashed in Gunnar's blue eyes but it was gone just as quickly as it had appeared, if it even appeared at all. These days I couldn't be absolutely certain.

"We have to stop this ring of armed robbers. One way or another," he said, his voice laced with determination.

I groaned but kept my mouth shut because this sounded a lot like murder, something I sure as shit didn't sign up for. I'd already done my time killing on behalf of other people, and I was done with that shit. Done and had the scars—mental and physical—to prove that shit. "You want 'em dead?"

"Not necessarily, but people like these robbers need to know that Opey is ours, and we are willing to protect it and the people in it." His expression was fierce, determined and at least Cruz and Wheeler were on his side.

"If it'll make you feel better Saint, we can talk to 'em first."

"Make me feel better? What the fuck kind of bullshit is that? We're vets, Gunnar. Ex-soldiers.

Marines. Ranchers. Sex club operators. We are not vigilantes and we're not fucking gangsters, are we?"

"No," his shoulders sank. "We're not."

"Maybe not," Wheeler stood and placed a big hand on Gunnar's shoulders, showing solidarity among the leadership. "But Gunnar is right about one thing, we can't let criminal activity in town go unpunished, not just because we'll take the blame, but because it'll end up on our fucking doorstep eventually."

"You believe that, Wheeler?" He was a straight shooter, whether we wanted to hear the truth or not, but I didn't like this crime talk.

He scoffed and looked me right in the eyes. "Yeah, Saint, I do. Think about if a non-club member found out about The Barn Door, a criminal in need of money. They could do a hell of a lot more than rob the place. They could blackmail every goddamn name in the book."

"Not to mention the MC shit," Cruz added. Unnecessarily.

Fuck. Wheeler was right. Gunnar and Cruz were right too. "I understand what you guys are saying but, I'm not sure if I'm up for this." I waited for the inevitable bullshit razzing from the guys or maybe something worse. Mocking.

The room fell silent, and I stared at the mud that had settled into the cracks of my black boots for so long I nearly missed the knowing looks the others shot each other, about me no doubt. Like I was some fucking head case they needed to watch and looked after like a goddamn infant.

"Saint, outside. Now."

No matter what else happened, Gunnar was the boss. I followed him outside, leaving the rest of the bunkhouse in total silence.

***

Five feet separated Gunnar and me but it might as well have been a gulf as wide as Texas. His steps were brisk, resolute. Angry. With dusty jeans and a ripped t-shirt, he looked more like a farmer than a biker, but his attitude was all biker. He stopped and put his hands on his hip with a deep, frustrated exhale.

"Help me out here, Saint. You said you wanted in the club, did all the work to do it, and now you have doubts."

"Not doubts, man. Just questions." I stopped right beside him and stared out at the sun kissed land with my arms folded over my chest. "This ain't the military, Gunnar. If I can't have questions, then this won't work."

There would never again be a time when I blindly followed someone's orders, especially when taking someone's life was involved.

"I'm not talking about that," he spat out angrily and looked at me.

"Then what the fuck are you talking about because I'm really confused."

He huffed a frustrated breath. "I'm talking about the thing we're all trying hard not to think about, Saint. Mitch is here and I really think you should talk to him."

"That's what this is about? I don't need to talk to anyone, Gunnar, but thanks for your concern."

"It's not just my concern, Saint. This is friendly advice. You're not doing well. Hardly sleeping, and you look like shit. You're not the first serviceman to suffer from PTSD, Saint. I hope you know that."

Of course I knew I wasn't so special as to be patient zero for PTSD, but I also knew that talking about it wouldn't make the memories or the dreams go away. "I do, thanks."

"So why are you so reluctant to talk about it?"

"I'm trying to move forward. That's what the ranch and the club and the Reckless Bastards is all about. Isn't it?" Moving on was the only way to keep my head above water from one day to the next, the only way forward was to try to forget the past.

"Maybe you're right, maybe I don't belong here. Hell, I don't even know how to ride a fucking bike."

He froze and turned slowly; eyes wide as saucers. "You *what*?"

"You heard me," I said reluctantly. It wasn't something I wanted to admit, but now that we were hashing shit out, now was as good a time as any. "I've never ridden a bike. A motorcycle. A hog."

Piercing blue eyes stared at me before he tilted his head back and barked out a laugh. "Holy shit man, you really can't ride?"

I shook my head, and he laughed even harder. Asshole.

"No wonder you're so freaked. Come on." He was already walking away before issuing the command.

I had to scramble to keep up with his long-legged stride. "Come on where?"

"We're gonna get you comfortable on a bike. Can't be in an MC without the motorcycle, Saint." He flashed a wide, genial smile and clapped his hands loud enough to echo in the field. "Let's go. We'll go to the northeast side of the property so no one else can see you fall on your scrawny little ass."

"Scrawny? I have a really nice ass I'll have you know." The only thing that I hadn't let go of since leaving the service was my dedication to physical fitness, and that was only because it was one hell of a stress reliever. And a great way to get two or three hours of sleep each night. If I could find a way to sleep without the nightmares, life might end up perfect.

Gunnar gave me a once over. "It's all right, but I've seen better," he said seriously, only laughing when I flipped him the middle finger.

"How is it that you've never ridden before?"

It was a fair question. "Grew up in New York and didn't even get a license to drive until just before I started basic training. Between the subway and cabs, I never had a need to learn and motorcycles aren't all that prevalent in the sand box."

"Smart ass," he grumbled. "Nothing feels better than all that horsepower at your fingertips. There's a certain amount of freedom on a bike. Just you, the machine, and the open fucking road. No worries. No problems. Just eating up the pavement."

He made it sound like a special kind of heaven, not just another method of transportation.

"Sounds better than a woman."

Gunnar laughed. "In some ways it is. Nothing is better than a hot beautiful woman, but this comes damn close." His smile was pure bliss, enough so that it sounded appealing. Damn appealing.

What the hell did I know about any of that? Women had never been anything more than a good time for me, a few hours to satisfy my physical needs—and theirs—but nothing more. I'd never been in love, never even lived with a woman. But the way Gunnar spoke about both of those things made me wonder if I was missing out on something important.

"Let's do it, then."

KB Winters

Chapter Two

Hazel

I had to get this job. Had to. Hell, I needed this job more than I've needed any of the other shitty jobs I've held in my twenty-six years of living. More than the greasy spoon diner where I waited tables while the middle-aged manager pretended that groping my ass was accidental. More than the fast food place where teenage girls gave head in the freezer to earn better shifts from the manager's greasy son. It was one more shitty job, but it paid cash money, which was helpful if I wanted to continue to have a roof over my head and food in my belly, which I did.

Not getting this job wasn't an option because I had no fall back plan. No loving parents waiting for me to return to the family fold or begging me to come home for a long overdue visit. Nope, all I had was a string of foster families who'd gotten a check for taking care of me. All of them had opted out of my care as soon as the checks stopped coming. So I was on my own. Completely and totally on my fucking own.

So yeah, I needed this job.

Badly.

I'd fished out my best pair of black jeans with the hole in one knee that hugged my toned thighs and ass just enough to let the interviewer see I was attractive enough. Fit enough. I tied my white blouse at the waist, a look that gave me even more up top than I actually possessed. Cheap black stilettos completed the look along with natural makeup and neat hair. It was the best I could do with my limited wardrobe. My personality and work experience would have to do the rest.

At the last minute I added a coat of Kiss Me Crazy red to my lips and stepped out of my jalopy of a car, ready to nail this fucking interview. The Barn Door was a discreet adult club. Reading between the lines, I figured it was some kind of sex club and I'd traded my normal interview outfit for something a little sexier. Maybe even a little trashy? It had to work.

WICKED

I took in several fortifying breaths, adjusted my minimal cleavage one last time before I opened the proverbial barn door and stepped inside a dimly lit security space with cameras situated on all sides. Top notch security, which was comforting. If I got the job. I waited alone while camera's whirred, and I stared at several locked doors. Nearly a minute later the door to one of the offices clicked, and I pulled it open easily and stepped inside an adult playhouse.

Leather and velvet or maybe it was suede, covered every surface. Shades of black and red and purples dominated the room, along with a long, dark wood bar gleaming with brass accents. Two cages hung suspended from the ceiling on my left, each of them big enough for people. Grown up people. Naked grown up people.

"We're not open," a deep voice sounded to my right, startling the shit out of me. I swiveled my head until I saw the man, tall with wide shoulders and a menacing glare I just bet he used with wild abandon.

"Good thing or I'd be very late for my interview. I'm Hazel and I have an appointment with someone named Joplin Saint."

His shoulders relaxed just a bit, and I wondered who he'd been expecting. "Hazel, good to meet you. I'm Gunnar, and I own this place. This man right here is the manager, Joplin Saint."

He clapped the other guy on the back as he took a step forward. I took a step back and he gave me a dark look, like I might be a piece of bad meat before he extended his hand.

"Right." I covered up my nervousness with a firm shake of my own. "Good to meet you Gunnar." I offered my hand to Joplin as well. "You, too."

"Yeah, you too," the manager mumbled, barely even sparing me a glance. That was just fine with me. Joplin was good looking with slightly unkempt light brown hair and jade green eyes that he probably used to hypnotize women into falling for his lines. He was over six feet with wide shoulders and a narrow waist that faded into square hips and muscled, denim-covered thighs.

Hopefully, he would be my boss so his looks would mean fuck all to me.

"Right." I stared at Joplin and then Gunnar, waiting for someone to speak. "Do you guys have questions?"

Gunnar chuckled. "Yeah, sorry today has been crazy already. Let's go back to the office and do this interview right."

Suddenly, alarm bells went off. What the hell kind of interview required me to be in a room with two big ass, strong ass men?

"Is that necessary? We can't do it here?"

Gunnar stopped and turned to me, studying me before he spoke. "No. Don't worry, no nudity or sex required for this job, Hazel."

Since beggars couldn't be choosers, I gave him a polite smile and a nod to lead the way before I slipped my hand into my purse and wrapped it around my pepper spray. Just in case.

The office surprised me. I'm not sure what I expected, but certainly not this statement that said The Barn Door was all business, a bright recessed light in the ceiling, a sleek metal desk with a leather office chair. Two metal chairs sat on the other side of the desk and behind them a dark sofa made me wonder why the hell they'd put a couch in there if they didn't expect any sex.

"Very minimalist," I said, waiting for my instructions.

Gunnar snorted and sat down on one of the metal chairs. I saw him send a discreet nod to Joplin. Interesting.

"That's one way of looking at it, Hazel. We've been open for a while, but the office is strictly utilitarian. We don't play around in here."

Play around? I bowed my head to indicate I understood and kept looking around the room, not because I was interested in the décor, but because there wasn't a damn thing else to look at except the two men stumbling through this interview. Still, I needed this job so I sat down in the other metal chair with my back straight, crossed my legs, and kept a polite but slightly mysterious smile on my face. "So?"

"Right." Joplin finally broke his stare with a few rapid blinks. "You don't have much bartending experience."

It wasn't a question, but I had practiced an answer on the way over. "No. The problem with working in bars is that I didn't know who a creep was until it was too late. Since this is an exclusive club, I'm hoping this place will be different." There was enough of the truth woven in that they wouldn't ask questions so I smiled through it, hoping they wouldn't ask more on that particular subject.

"What's your cocktail knowledge?" Joplin stared right at me as though I was about to reveal the secrets of the universe and I stumbled. Dammit.

"Pretty substantial. I can make pretty much anything from a margarita to a Manhattan, a Whiskey or Pisco Sour too. Most of the martini style drinks, some classics and a long list of one-offs."

I wasn't sure if that came off as cocky or competent, but I figured a secluded adult club like this would have high-end clientele who knew their shit.

Gunnar snorted and shook his head. "Pisco Sour? Did you just make that up?"

I flashed my best sexy but untouchable bartender smile. "Pisco, egg white, lemon juice and simple syrup." He still wasn't convinced. "Google it."

He pulled out his phone and did, then flashed a grin at Joplin before swinging that all seeing gaze back to me. "Slow Screw Up Against the Wall."

My lips curled in the spirit of competition. "Vodka, Sloe gin, SoCo, OJ and...Galliano."

"Damn, you're good. Criminal record?"

"Nope." Thank fuck for that. Most of the other fosters I knew ended up in juvie or jail before they aged out of the system, not because they were bad but because life was damn hard when they'd been rejected by the people meant to love them forever.

Gunnar's smile faded slowly and he leaned forward. "You do know what kind of club this is Hazel?" I nodded and his shoulders relaxed, making me wonder how the other applicants had reacted. Terribly, I hoped.

"Good. The job is for front bartender but sometimes we might need you to take the back room if you're up for it. But under no circumstances do you have to get sexy or anything with anyone. Clients or employees. Got it?"

"Sure." He was so serious, gravely so, that it kind of warmed some of the ice on the outer layer of my barriers. A little. "Thanks for saying it, anyway."

"Good. And if we hire you, report any inappropriate behavior to me or Saint, here. No touching allowed."

"Me or the clients?" Shit, what possessed me to ask *that* question? Now they would think I was some kind of perv—or worse.

Gunnar laughed and Joplin didn't.

"Touch or indulge if you want. Off the clock though. When would you be available to start?"

"Yesterday?"

Gunnar's broad shoulders fell just a little more.

"Great. We have a few more interviews today, but we'll make a decision by tomorrow." He stood and left the room, the rest of us apparently forgotten.

"Do you have any more questions, Mr. Saint?"

His green eyes had a faraway look about them, not like someone daydreaming but someone who couldn't look away from whatever it was they saw. I didn't want to bother him, but I couldn't exactly leave now, could I? No, I couldn't.

I placed a hand on his and sat there as one minute ticked by and then two. Three. Five. Eight. "Mr. Saint?"

His eyes blinked slow at first, then faster like little hummingbird wings, revealing the barest hint of his oddly colored green eyes. "What are you still doing here?"

"Gunnar just left and you were uhm, not listening. So I waited," I said and tried to discreetly remove my hand, but that only drew *more* attention to the inappropriate touching. "I need this job, and I wanted to make sure all of your questions were answered." I hoped that didn't sound as sexual to him as it did to my own ears because yeah, the guy was hot, but I needed a job more than I needed a man.

Then again it had been months since I'd been fucked properly.

"I hear a bit of accent in your voice. You from here?"

That's what he wanted to talk about? "Uh, yeah. I lived most of my life in Arkansas, and I've lived around here for about a year, so a southern girl, I guess." It was a strange question that left me feeling unsettled, but it was easy enough to answer. And still, I smiled.

Joplin stood and took a step back. "I think that's it, Hazel. If I have more questions I'll give you a call."

"Okay, thanks Mr. Saint. Have a good one." I tossed him a half-hearted wave and made my way down the dark hall and to the front room and back out into the overcast day. It was hard to read this interview. At a sex club.

With two guys so normal they looked like cops. Undercover cops sure, but still cops. Gunnar seemed impressed by my cocktail knowledge but Joplin didn't seem too impressed about anything, not to mention I was pretty sure he'd gotten the wrong idea about me hanging around.

If I did get the job I would have to be more careful. Keep my head down, eyes averted and ears open. *Back against the wall.*

Fuck, I hoped I'd get the job.

Chapter Three

Saint

Gunnar leaned over to me across the front bar. "Hazel is obviously the best candidate. She knows her drinks and she's good eye candy for the members." Excitement turned his blue eyes almost black. "What did you think?"

What did I think? That was a good damn question. The woman had left me feeling...*something*. I couldn't name it and didn't want to think about Hazel. Maybe it was all that pale creamy skin with her shockingly dark brown eyes and darker hair. Or maybe it was the deep-seated pain I saw in her eyes that she couldn't conceal.

"She knows a few drinks," I said as if I didn't care one way or the other.

Gunnar frowned. "What's the problem, Saint?"

I shrugged because I had no fucking clue. "No problem, but...isn't she kind of young for the main bar?"

"That's exactly why I want her. She knows a lot of drink recipes, and she looks good, which means customers will spend a lot of money just trying to get some alone time with her."

His excitement was almost contagious. Almost. Except all I could think about was a woman like Hazel would get eaten alive in a place like this. Chewed up, spit out, and forgotten about before she was could head for the door.

It was a bad idea, a really bad one for a variety of reasons. But Gunnar was right about one thing. She'd do a good job, not to mention she said she needed the job.

I shrugged. "Fine. Let's hire her."

"Great," he said and pushed away from the bar. "I've got some calls to make back at my office, but don't forget about later."

Then he was gone before I could say anything else.

Gunnar was determined to not just heal me but to turn me into a badass, motorcycle riding biker. There were worse things I could've been, and at least Gunnar gave a damn about my well-being. Still didn't mean I was ready to become a biker or a vigilante, but everyone on Hardtail Ranch was a work in progress.

"Enough," I growled to myself, frustrated that my mind continued to wander whether I wanted it to or not. It was damn annoying, and I needed to get it under control if I had a chance in hell of doing a good job as manager of this club. Gunnar put his trust in me, and I planned to make sure he never fucking regretted it. Which meant I needed to stop dicking around and place a call.

To Hazel.

Thankfully, the phone rolled to voicemail. "This is Hazel, leave a message," it said. Short and simple, no frills, just like the woman herself. Even dressed to impress yesterday, she'd kept it simple with sexy, figure-hugging jeans and a blouse that gave her peekaboo cleavage.

"Hey, uh, Hazel. This is Joplin Saint from The Barn Door. I'm calling to let you know the job is yours, if you want it." I stumbled over my words and got the fuck off the phone as fast as I could, keeping my words civil and distant. I should have prepared what I wanted to say first, but lack of sleep was fucking with me and I found it damn near impossible to focus.

Why was Hazel screwing with my peace of mind? There was something about her I couldn't shake, and it had nothing to do with her beauty. She'd caught me staring at her, but instead of batting her eyelashes or poking her chest out to ensure she got the job, she looked away. At first. Then I drifted off to the desert thousands of miles and a whole fucking world away, to a time when my whole world had been torn apart by a bunch of religious-fucking-zealots. I hated going back there but I couldn't control where my mind visited. And when I came back, Hazel appeared in front of me, her small hand soft and delicate on top of mine. The worst part was that I *did* feel comfort and warmth coming from her, a kind of compassionate touch that was only meant to soothe.

WICKED

She was a damned enigma with her polite but distant smile. Her brown eyes that for all their light and life couldn't hide some kind of suffering. She'd painted them with a shimmery green color and outlined them with thick black eyeliner that made them look so huge and dark it was all I could do not to stare into them. Her pale milky skin under the dark curtain of hair and long lashes gave her an innocent appeal that belied the very grown up pain she clearly carried.

I snorted out a laugh at that. Me, diagnosing someone else's pain while avoiding mine like a blind man.

I had to stop fucking around and thinking about Hazel, though, because it turned out that running a club was a big damn job. It wasn't just employees I had to worry about with schedules and benefits and paychecks and discipline, but also club inventory that went a lot further than booze. The Barn Door kept free condoms and lube on hand for all members, a huge number of sex toys for purchase, which then had to be replaced. There was social media, which thankfully

Peaches had taken over along with the club newsletter that announced weekly special-themed events.

No matter how much I complained to myself, I appreciated the hell out of this job. It kept me busy and more importantly, it kept my mind occupied enough that I didn't think about the guys, the friends, the brothers who hadn't made it home with me. Higgs, Jank, and Pony Boy were my brothers, the closest thing left to family I had. And they were all rotting away in pine boxes in D.C.

Bullshit, that's what it was.

***

"Ready?" Gunnar's voice sounded behind me. I turned quickly, hand at my side in search of what I no longer kept there.

"Shit man, don't sneak up on me like that." I sent him a narrow-eyed glare, but the asshole just grinned in reply. "Ready for what?"

Gunnar looked down at his bike, all leather and chrome. And noise. His gaze flicked back to mine with one brown brow arched in question. "Motorcycle lessons."

I groaned. "I got a hang of the basics." That much was true. I had the controls memorized but it would take some time before I got used to the hand controls.

"Good, but you'll need more than that to ride beside me. And to get your license." He laughed when another groan escaped. "You can't be out here riding dirty, Saint. We're trying to limit our contact with the cops."

"Oh, is that how it works?" My voice dripped with sarcasm, which brought a flash of surprise to his eyes.

"Smartass." I walked beside Gunnar toward the big empty field with soft grass that provided plenty of cushioning for an inexperienced rider like me.

The lesson, like the first one, went well. I wasn't comfortable on a bike, yet, but I would be. This was part of being in the MC, being one of the Reckless

Bastards. Being a brother. The longer we stayed at it, the more comfortable, the more confident I became.

"It's starting to feel natural," I said as we parked the bikes, and I took off my helmet.

"Good," Gunnar said, slapping my shoulder. "You should get out here every day for an hour or more until you feel confident. Long distance rides can be brutal and with Hardtail being out in Bum-fuck Egypt, most rides will be long as hell."

I nodded and stared at the machine next to me, cold and intimidating. The keys to some other type of freedom.

"So, Saint," he said as we walked back to the Barn. "Have you given any more thought to the armed robbers situation?"

"I've thought about little else, Gunnar." But I still hadn't reached any decision. Unfortunately. "Didn't you come here to get away from this kind of shit, Gunnar? To get Maisie away from it?"

WICKED

I didn't mean to be an asshole, but that was all he spent the first few months in Opey talking about, keeping danger and shit away from his sister.

"I did, but this is inevitable, Saint. We have to hit them before they hit us because trust me, they will get around to us eventually."

I could see that Gunnar believed that, but to me it sounded eerily familiar.

"So what you're saying is that they'll greet us as liberators?"

He groaned and shook his head, raking a hand through his thick hair. "Is that how I sound?"

I shrugged. "A little. So, tell me, what made you come out here and build a sex club?"

"Adult entertainment, Saint." He chuckled and ran his hand across his stubble. "Once I liquidated everything in Mayhem with the original Bastards, I wanted to come out here and relax. With Maisie. I met this real estate agent, Leah, Lorna, can't even remember her name but she had the hook ups."

"For a sex—I mean, *adult* club? How do you get hook ups for that? Was she an madame or something?" This was all new to me, but it paid well. And I didn't have to partake.

"She'd told me they used to have an adult club over in Vance, but the owner died and they closed it up. I got with the Mayor and city council and they were all for it. Apparently, the Mayor and his wife have some serious kink. Gave me some good tax breaks, too, so here we are."

"Cool. So about the robberies, you really want to take that on? With Maisie and all?" I asked.

"No, Saint, I don't. But we have to come up with something."

I didn't want to be a fucking vigilante, but Wheeler's words kept bouncing around in my mind.

"I'm not sure I can do this." Not sure I even had the guts to pull a trigger anymore, honestly.

Gunnar sent me a knowing smile. "If only there was a way to help you with that." His sarcasm wasn't lost on me.

I flipped him off while he continued to laugh at my every fall, every stumble. But when the motorcycle lesson was over, I called Wheeler's brother Mitch, to make an appointment.

To talk.

KB Winters

Chapter Four

Hazel

Eating instant noodle soup was getting old. Too salty with almost no variety, the only thing it had going for it was that it was dirt cheap and fairly low in calories. Being poor was doing wonders for my waistline, so that was a bonus. Plus, having a smaller ass meant the springs in the sofa didn't dig uncomfortably into my butt cheeks and also meant the bed didn't squeak as much as it used to when I tossed and turned all night.

But this was home. My home. I'd spent all day yesterday and most of today here trying to get a job. I needed to keep paying too much of my hard-earned money on rent for this place. The off-white paint was chipped in at least ten thousand different spots, and a brown stain in the corner seemed to grow larger by the day, but the landlord wasn't big on repairs. Or complaints. Or anything but collecting the rent on time. Still, the rent was cheap-*ish* and the building was relatively safe, at least when the neighbors didn't leave the front door unlocked because they were too fucking lazy to bring their keys. It was an ongoing battle, since I always made sure the door was closed and locked, no matter how I found it.

Okay, the place wasn't much, I knew. I'd furnished it with crappy, faded blue furniture, a 19-inch flat screen along with a few pots and pans and other dishes, a full size bed and some clothes. But all of it was mine, and I would protect it any way I could. From anyone who threatened it.

Story of my goddamn life.

I tossed the Styrofoam container into the trash and grabbed my phone from the charger, noticing a few missed calls and messages. The first voice was the one I most wanted to hear. "Hey, uh, Hazel. This is Joplin Saint from The Barn Door. I'm calling to let you know the job is yours, if you want it."

If I wanted it? There was no damn question that I wanted it. The job paid five bucks more per hour than any of the others I'd interviewed for this past week. I grabbed my phone and returned the call immediately. My excitement, as always, was dampened by the fact that he didn't pick up, and until he did, the job wasn't mine. Not really. I called back and this time left a message.

"Joplin this is Hazel Greer, and I would love the job." I knew the dance before I could start work. The paperwork to complete, IDs to photocopy and tax forms to fill out.

"But I got the job."

The words seemed more real when they were spoken out loud. "I got the job. I got the fucking job!" Excitement bubbled to the surface as I clutched my phone in my hand, wishing like hell I had someone to celebrate with. I didn't have those kinds of connections anymore. I used to have them back when I was a naïve teenager who thought the foster families that took me in actually gave a fuck about me, but life and experience had cured me of that pipedream. Quickly.

But I still had Jessie. She was my best friend from foster care. The other kids we'd been in the system with were scattered across the globe, living on different continents, locked up in prison, serving in the military or simply just trying to hide from their pasts.

I had plenty of neighbors, but they weren't friends because I wasn't friendly. Not to the couple on my left who seemed to spend all of their free time fucking, not the older couple to the right of me who smoked weed and danced to Big Band music every night after dinner. That meant it was just me and myself alone to celebrate dodging homelessness.

This month, anyway.

I punched in the speed dial to Jessie. Shit. Voicemail. "Hey girl I've got some great news! Call me when you get a chance." I hit the end button and sighed. Jessie was always busy with her kids. She had a great life now.

And maybe I did, too.

Now that I had a job it was time to look at my budget, see what I had to work with until my first paycheck came. My two hundred bucks in the bank would have to last until then, but I hoped this exclusive club meant big fat tips, the kind that could buy late night snacks and maybe a beer after work.

The phone rang, and I answered immediately. "Hello?"

"Hazel? This is Joplin." He was so stiff and formal I was put off, and since he couldn't see me, I shrugged.

"Hi, Joplin. How's it going?"

"It's, uhm, going." Okay so he wasn't a big conversationalist. "You can come in any time before seven today to complete your paperwork, but we need you to start tomorrow night. Will that be a problem?"

"Not at all." Tomorrow I'd have a job again, which meant I could buy a few groceries after completing my paperwork. "I'll see you soon, Joplin."

"Bring I.D.," he growled into the phone.

I rolled my eyes, ignoring his attitude. "Anything else, Boss?"

"No." His voice was low and deep, almost angry. He ended the call abruptly, but all I could do was grin. The man was surly as hell and just as quiet. Handsome. Tortured. He had secrets, that much was sure, but I wasn't in the market for a mysterious tortured man with a stick up his ass. Hell, I wasn't in the market at all.

And he was my boss, so totally off limits.

I rushed over to The Barn Door to take the grand tour and fill out all of the necessary paperwork before they changed their mind.

***

Standing in front of the two dollar full-length mirror I'd found at a rummage sale, I gave myself a once over, slightly impressed that I'd managed to pull myself together halfway decently. The little black dress used to fit a little bit better, but things had been more famine than feast lately and the dress was a little loose in all the wrong places.

It was times like this that I wished I placed more importance on creating connections because it would be really nice to have a friend I could borrow a dress from for tonight or get some feedback on the current outfit. Hell, if I had a few friends I might invite them along to use my employee pass. My *free* employee pass to The Barn Door. And since I didn't start work until tomorrow night, I planned to take full advantage of tonight.

Discreetly.

I wanted to go and get rid of some of the stress hanging around my shoulders that made me look older than my twenty-six years. However, I didn't want this to be an open invitation to all the men I worked with. The women too, since I didn't know any of them or how they rolled. They could be complete bitches for all I knew. That was why I wore extra heavy makeup and a short blonde bob wig, hoping it was enough to hide my identity from everyone but the dude at the door.

Luckily for me, when I showed up at the club, the guy at the door didn't recognize me. He didn't bat an eyelash as he scanned the card and let me into the club. The music was so loud, so pulsing that I couldn't hear myself think, couldn't feel the rush of blood through my veins, and that was exactly what I was after. A night full of distractions and maybe an orgasm or two.

But first, I needed a drink. Just one drink to loosen me up and put an appropriate haze on the evening. Since the bar I would be manning tomorrow was closest, I stood at the edge and waited for the gorgeous bartender to wait on me. He was big as shit with wide shoulders, long brown hair and a scruffy beard that said he wasn't ashamed to get down and dirty. "What can I get ya, sweetheart?"

Yeah, I'd bet my next paycheck he was ten kinds of trouble, twenty on Saturday.

"An old fashioned, please." He blinked, clearly unaware of the drink.

"Help me out honey, our new bartender doesn't start until tomorrow."

All right, then. "Put a sugar cube in a glass and let the bitters drip with a splash of plain water, muddle until its dissolved. Add ice and pour an ounce and a half of bourbon in and serve." The guy nodded and motioned for me to follow him to the other end of the bar and I did.

"I'm Slayer," he said, his tone friendly and open as he scanned the shelves for bourbon and bitters. If he was helping out, then chances were he was friends with Gunnar or Joplin. Maybe even had a different job here at the club. "That wig isn't hiding shit, honey."

His words registered a half a beat late and I blinked up at him. "Excuse me?"

"The blonde wig. It's hot, but it's not doing a damn thing to hide who you are."

"What?" I shouted to him over the thumping bass.

He tossed his head back and laughed, showing off full lips, a strong chin and an Adam's apple that would have any woman licking her lips. "It's called being discreet. Hazel."

I took a step back, eyes wide and suddenly feeling like I'd walked into the fucking Twilight Zone. "Forget the drink. Thanks." So much for a night of relaxation.

"Hey! Wait! I work the ranch and help out here sometimes." His hand landed on my shoulder, and I shrugged him off because big and handsome or not, he was a stranger. "Sorry."

"That doesn't explain how you know my name."

He sighed. "I saw you when you came in earlier to fill out your paperwork. Asked Gunnar who you were."

"Well fuck me."

His chuckle sounded rich and deep, even with the dance beat vibrating every molecule of my body. "I've seen worse. You don't even look legal."

"Thanks," I glared.

Slayer laughed again. "Anytime. I tell you what, come monitor the drink and I promise not to tell anyone you're here."

"Deal."

WICKED

Only time would tell if Slayer was someone I could trust, but if he did tell, it was no big deal. My private life was my own, dammit.

"Is it always like this?" The place was already pretty damn packed, at least the dance floor was, but there wasn't a whole lot of dancing. Mostly everyone was half-naked or more, bumping and grinding on one another. It was foreplay to music, and I had no problem with that.

"Friday and Saturday are the craziest," he said, nodding at the sugar cube in the glass, sighing when I gave a satisfied nod. "We'll throw you right into the deep end. Old Fashioned."

"Thanks Slayer. You might have a future as a bartender after all." I grabbed the glass, took a sip and sauntered off, determined to enjoy my night for the next couple of hours.

With the bourbon flowing through my veins, the sexy Latin dance beat made my hips swirl with every step as the music soaked into my bloodstream. The back dance floor, complete with a six-foot high stage, was even more crowded than the front. The bar was three people deep, stopping me dead in my tracks.

"Nope." I turned away down another dimly lit hall that led to a spiral stairway with a soft velvet bannister, which hadn't been part of the new employee tour.

Big black doors on each side of the hallway gave the downstairs area an eerie, horror movie vibe. Until I stopped in front of what looked like a big ass window and pressed the black button on the wall, because holy fucking shit, this is what I came here for.

A woman lay spread-eagle on a bed, bound by her hands and ankles with silk scarves, a black blindfold covering her eyes so she could feel everything. Four men stood around the bed, stroking already hard cocks and looking at her with fire in their eyes. The first guy knelt beside the bed and swiped his tongue over one dusky pink nipple and the woman gasped and arched into him.

He laughed.

The man opposite him did the same while the third stretched half on and half off the bed, shoulders pushing her legs so far apart I could see the slickness on her pussy lips from here.

"You're so fuckin' wet," he growled a second before he closed his eyes and put his mouth on her, feasting on her pussy like she was a seven-course gourmet meal. It was enough to make a girl jealous.

To make a girl shiver with desire. Hell, who am I kidding, my pussy was so wet and aching and that was *before* the fourth guy straddled her shoulders and fed her his cock.

A strangled groan escaped, and I took a step back before I did something foolish before my job technically started. I liked to wait until I had something to lose before I fucked up irrevocably. But fuck, I'd love to be in her position.

I wandered to the next room, set up strictly for those who liked to be watched, with auditorium seats all around a big stage with an even bigger bed.

Inside another room I happened upon a man and two women. One of the women was strapped naked to a St. Andrew's Cross, with a ball gag in her mouth. She shivered while the couple knelt before her, giving her a two-tongue salute. All she could do was take the erotic torture and let her moans do all the work, tied as she was to the structure. The scene was enough to make me wish I'd left my panties at home because they were soaked, and I hadn't even made it to the end of the hall yet.

I didn't join in with any of the kinky fun being had all around me, but I was happy to find this place. *My* place. The other rooms had me intrigued enough to keep going but when I got to the final room, the big velvet room, I couldn't help but stop.

Watch.

Enjoy.

The whole group was naked, a rainbow of skin tones ranging from the palest white to the darkest mahogany and every shade in between from English rose to butterscotch brown: three women and four men in various stages of ecstasy. One woman sat on a man's face, rolling and grinding her hips while she took a cock down her throat. They were all connected by one erotic act or another. Another woman was flat on her back while the redhead ate her out and took a cock from behind, moaning into her pussy.

The door wasn't open but even still, I swear I could inhale the scent of sex in the air. Damp skin, the thick musk of arousal and sweat, the desperate strain to receive more pleasure, it all had a unique scent. The kind that stuck to your skin and your hair, didn't go away for days and days.

As much as my fingers itched to join in, to strip down and close my eyes and let pleasure take me over, though it was exactly what I needed, I knew it was too soon.

I wasn't ready.

But when I was ready, this room was where I would start.

KB Winters

Chapter Five

Saint

The dream was back. It was always the same fucking dream, too. I was back in Afghanistan with my squad. Jerry "Jank" Jankowski was the guy in charge. He only acted like a Staff Sergeant when he sat beside Higgs barking out orders and directions.

Derek "Higgs" Higgins was my best friend and the guy behind the wheel of the tank as we traipsed all over the goddamn desert in search of invisible enemies. Pony Boy was what we called the hired gun. The man could handle anything with a firing pin or trigger. He got his nickname thanks to his love of jeans, white t-shirts, and black leather jackets. Pony Boy was our eyes and ears, and I was the intel, talking to villagers and police officers alike trying to keep the area safe.

Usually we had another guy with us called Polo, a blue blood Army legacy who spoke eight different languages. He'd been given to another unit with an embedded journalist that day.

Lucky bastard.

We drove along the dirt road in the southwest part of the country that bordered Pakistan, necks on a swivel on our way to look into a compound rumored to belong to a terrorist the U.S. government had deemed a BFD.

"What makes this asshole a big fucking deal, anyway?" Higgs shouted the question over one of Jank's crude jokes.

Jank rolled his eyes, insulted someone had stepped on his salty joke. "The fact that he's an explosives expert and a former chemistry professor. Allegedly."

"Shit." Pony Boy said the words we were all thinking. "Sounds like a fuckin' wild goose chase to me," he said and returned to his position behind the gun.

"He ain't wrong," I added when the tank fell silent. "This compound is made up of half a dozen structures with underground tunnels that lead to the mountains about forty kilometers away."

From the beginning this sounded like a shit show, but watching it play in a dream was absolute fucking torture because I knew how it would all end. Knew that Pony Boy was right.

Knew that in the end, none of that knowledge or righteousness mattered one fucking bit.

We were about ten kilometers from the compound when Pony Boy's voice rang out. "Think I caught a glare at four o'clock," he shouted. "I'm checking it out." Those were Pony Boy's the last words before the shooting began.

It came suddenly, the gunshots fired from a distance, which meant the glare Pony Boy saw was exactly what he thought it was. Trouble for our squad, the kind of trouble that usually ended with no survivors or a bunch of damn medals.

The shots came from the right. At first. When bullets went flying, it didn't matter than that the tank was thick enough to withstand the onslaught, I fucking dropped down as far as I could while I readied my weapon.

"I got two on the ridge at two o'clock!" There were two men in white, one with a... "Fuck! RPG!"

We were hit hard as fuck from the right but we were still upright and Higgs still had control of the vehicle. "Pony Boy, you all right?"

A long silence fell over the valley, at least it felt long but it was only a matter of seconds before more bullets went flying right at us. Jank was hit first and immediately slumped over.

"Fuck, they got Jank!"

Higgs freaked out but he kept driving, glancing occasionally at our Sergeant and his lifeless eyes. "Jank! Fuck!"

From above, Pony Boy kept shooting and shooting, the hot shells falling everywhere, and that day was well over one hundred degrees even in the fucking shade, but it was nothing compared to those casings.

Another RPG sounded in the distance and we couldn't do anything in this position but brace ourselves for impact. When it came, the whole tank slid about twenty feet before tipping into a ditch, leaving us completely immobile.

Higgs and I jumped out and rounded the tank, using it for cover once we made sure there were no other shooters on our side of the valley. When Pony Boy didn't join us, I knew something was wrong.

"I'll check on Pony," I told Higgs and patted his shoulder.

"I'll hold these fuckers. See if you can get Command on the line."

I nodded my agreement, but my focus on was our potentially fallen man and when I found him, I knew what real terror was. Nearly split in half from the impact of the tank tipping over, Pony Boy stared up at the sun with blank eyes as all the blood drained from his body.

"Fuck! No, no, no." This couldn't be happening, not Pony Boy. Not today. Not fucking today.

"Get your ass back here, Saint!"

Higgs was on his own and outgunned and now it was just the two of us.

"Pony Boy's gone. Gruesome shit. Let's get these fuckers." It was the kind of blind rage they tried to train out of me during my time in the military, that instinct to seek revenge at all costs. It was a human trait but also deadly.

"Fuck, yeah," Higgs shouted back, an angry wild-eyed grin on his face. With our weapons aimed across the valley, we used all the ammo we could to stop them from advancing on us.

"I'm out," Higgs announced when the shooting had stopped again.

"Fuck. Check Jank and Pony." It was macabre but that was war. It wasn't pretty or civil. It was violent and brutal and no one got out unscathed.

The next thing I remembered was Higgs crying out and me rushing to his side. "I'm hit, Saint."

"I see that, Captain Obvious. Where?" Jank's blood was all over him, making it damn difficult to see which blood was his and where it came from.

"Too. Many." His words were already labored and before I could get his jacket off to check him, he coughed up blood right in my face, all down my uniform. Grabbing him by the collar, I dragged Higgs behind the tank when those fuckers started shooting again.

I had to return fire. It was the only way we'd have a chance in hell of getting out of there alive. When I looked back at Higgs, he was face down in the sand. Unmoving.

"Shit, Higgs. Stay with me!" I remember dropping down to my knees to flip him over, making sure he wasn't choking on his own blood or vomit, but it wasn't Higgs.

This time it wasn't fucking Higgs. It was Hazel, her coal black eyes just as lifeless as Pony Boy and Jank's.

"What the fuck?" It was that thought, that exclamation that had my eyes snapping open as a scream was ripped from my throat.

"Fuck!" I looked around the bunkhouse, happy to see that everyone else was still asleep.

There was no point in me trying to get back to sleep because after that fucking nightmare, I'd be lucky if I fell asleep tomorrow night. Or the night after that.

Creeping to the small kitchen inside the bunkhouse, I opened the fridge, hoping that a late night snack would help me relax enough to get back to sleep. Unlikely, but I had nothing else.

Warm milk was supposed to work but who the fuck drank warm milk, anymore?

"Fuck that." I spotted a bottle of Jack on top of the fridge and grabbed it along with a glass and headed outside. There was something about Hardtail Ranch that soothed me at moments like this. I'd been here a little over a year and tonight was the eighth time the nightmare had jolted me awake.

The nightmare itself was unsettling as fuck, but the strange twist of the new bartender had me feeling uneasy. Was that a subconscious warning that Hazel herself was trouble or was it more ominous than that? Was she in trouble or running from trouble? That would explain the pain in her eyes, but I didn't know the woman, didn't know shit about her or her pain. Or, if that even was pain I saw.

I couldn't worry about Hazel, not as anything more than an employee. I had enough of my own shit going on that I didn't need to go in search of damsels in need of saving. I sure as shit was nobody's hero.

But the dream had made one thing clear. Gunnar was right. It was time for me to talk to Mitch.

"I'm surprised you didn't cancel this time." Mitch used his words as an opening to get me to open up, not as a way to get under my skin which I appreciated.

"Me too, honestly." I'd made an appointment last week and canceled an hour before I was scheduled to meet with him. It was a dick move, but a man had to do what was right for him, when it was right.

Mitch nodded, his kind blue eyes holding mine. "What changed?"

There it was, the reason I didn't do shrinks. They were like fucking psychics, reading your mind and your thoughts. Forcing you to talk about shit better left dead and buried.

"Changed? Nothing, not really." That wasn't a lie. "Same nightmare I've been having on and off for a few years."

"Want to tell me about it?"

WICKED

Mitch looked just like Wheeler, maybe less pretty because he dressed like an accountant or a suburban dad, but they had the same brown hair and the same blue eyes. Where they differed was demeanor. Mitch was calm and steady as a rock. Patient.

"Not really, but isn't that why I'm here?" I rubbed my palms up and down my thighs to get rid of the sweat.

"You're here because you need some kind of help, but there's no preset path to that help. How about you tell me what about the nightmare last night was different?"

"Who says it was different?"

"You're here. Something scared you."

Right again. "It was the same nightmare. Me and Jank and Higgs and Pony Boy. Everything played out the way it always did but then..."

I couldn't even say it out loud. What the fuck did it mean? Was I losing my mind?

"Joplin, relax." His words brought me back from the spiral I was headed down. When our gazes connected, he smiled. "Then?"

"I turned Higgs over the way I always do, but when I turned him over last night he was…Hazel." The fucking bartender. My employee. A stranger.

"Is Hazel a sister or girlfriend?"

"No, she's the new bartender at The Barn Door."

"Oh." Mitch looked as dumbfounded as I felt.

"Exactly, it's weird as fuck, right? Why was she there? Is my subconscious trying to tell me something?" Did I even believe in subconscious messages?

"Possibly." He suppressed a chuckle at the glare I shot him. "I know it's not what you want to hear Joplin, but we won't know what it's about until we start talking."

"What's with you shrinks and talking?"

WICKED

Mitch did nothing to hide his amusement this time. "It's called talk therapy for a reason. If you don't want to talk about the nightmare, tell me about your job at The Barn Door. How do you like it?"

Wasn't that a loaded question? "I like it just fine."

"A perfect non-answer." He smiled again, completely unmoved by my attitude. The bastard.

I shrugged. "It's a nice distraction from my own thoughts. Memories. Nightmares and shit I would rather not talk about. Keeps me busy."

Mitch nodded slowly, like he was thinking, and I knew it didn't bode well for me. "Tell me about a good memory you have with the guys in your unit."

"I have plenty of good memories," I insisted.

"Good, tell me one."

He didn't dare smile, but with the smugness that radiated off him, he might as well have smiled.

I didn't answer right away, so he pressed me. "Just one. Should be easy."

Yeah, it should've been but it wasn't. I'd worked the last year or so to forget everything. The smiles and the laughter at the inappropriate jokes, the Yo Mama jokes that were a big hit with Pony Boy and Jank. I tried to forget it all, but what no one told me about war is just how deep the memories—good and bad—would become ingrained into me. They become a part of the fabric of who I was, once the war was over. I couldn't erase the memories. I tried. "You're a real bastard, you know that right?"

Mitch shrugged. "I've been called worse. I'm still waiting on that good memory, Saint."

Shit. Looked like I wouldn't get out of this session unscathed.

"All right." If Mitch wanted a memory then I'd give him one. "We were on leave and decided to head up to Iceland. Ever been?"

"Nowhere close to it. Nice?"

I nodded. "It was surprisingly beautiful but cold. We should've done our research before we landed because we were not prepared for that kind of cold. We turned it into a game."

He sat there with a blank expression on his face but I could sense his need to lean in, to learn more. "We all tried to gather enough cold weather supplies. Whoever came in last place had to pay for dinner and drinks the whole trip."

Mitch whistled. "Sounds expensive."

"It was only two full days of leave, but yeah it was pricey."

His eyes widened in surprise. "You lost?"

"Hell, yeah. Jank managed to find Icelandic soldiers who outfitted us with everything. Higgs used his good looks to get scarves, gloves and hats from a group of widows who knit for soldiers all around the world, leaving me and Pony Boy with nothing but some thick socks and a bottle of Absinthe. Horrible shit but effective against the cold."

A smile touched my lips at the memory, how we all worked together to make sure the trip was a fun one.

"Sounds like a good time."

"It was. Saw an active volcano and danced with plenty of pretty Icelandic women. Never saw so many blondes in my life."

We'd taken that trip about seven months before it all went to shit, one of the last good memories I had with my guys away from the fucking warzone. After that day it was all recon and cleanup missions mostly with the occasional rescue tossed in just to keep us on our toes.

"It was a great fucking time."

"Sounds like it was." Mitch's words hung in the air for a long time, and I stared back at him, not really seeing Mitch, just a slideshow of laughing and smiling faces.

"Next time you feel your memories going to that day, try to focus on this memory instead. I know it won't be easy," he said, beating me to the punch. "But you won't know if you don't try."

"Fine, I'll try. Anything else?"

"Tell me about Hazel. About work." His tone was quiet and unassuming, as usual, but there was a hint of something else I couldn't put my finger on. Yet.

There was nothing to tell about Hazel other than she was good at her job. Knew enough drinks to impress the good ol' boys and more importantly, to keep them buying drinks. And damn if these southern boys couldn't handle their liquor.

"Work is good, mostly logistics and planning which happens to be my strong suit. Not much else to tell."

"Are you seeing anyone?"

"Not at the moment. I haven't had much time with The Barn Door and all the other shit going on in my life right now."

The Reckless Bastards thing gave me pause, a big goddamn pause, but I was a man of my word. That didn't mean I was down for vigilante justice, but the pragmatist in me couldn't deny that Gunnar's arguments made sense.

"How are you feeling about the…other stuff?"

My lips quirked into an appreciative smile. "Hesitant. I'm not sure I…never mind." I couldn't talk about this, not with Mitch when his brother was the goddamn VP, and definitely not now. "I'm feeling fine, just questioning myself and my…condition."

I hated saying that shit just like I hated those four fucking letters. They were like a brand, a word people whispered in polite company because it was just too horrible to say at a normal volume. They didn't know the fucking half of it. "Thanks, Doc. I'll, uh, see you soon."

"I hope that's true. You made progress today. It will only continue if you do."

"I hear ya." I did, and I understood what he was saying, I just wasn't sure if I was ready to make more progress than that. The more I talked about it, the more I thought about it and that was a vicious damn cycle that might land me in an VA hospital. Not gonna happen.

WICKED

I stood, said my goodbye and made my way back to the bunkhouse to change before heading to The Barn Door for the night.

Chapter Six

Hazel

I didn't have to be at work until ten, so I showed up a little early and went back to that room. There was something deep and dark and visceral about watching a group of strangers fuck. It was primal, bodies slick with sweat, faces contorted into varying stages of ecstasy as every man and woman sought their own pleasure while helping bring about someone else's.

At first glance it seemed selfish, just bodies fucking away at each other looking to get off by any means necessary, but a good orgy had a depth to it that most people couldn't understand. Right now it looked like the women were just being used, just fuck holes for four horny cocks, but that was not what I saw when I took it all in.

What I saw was those women giving the men a great deal of trust. Trust that his cock won't go so far down her throat that she choked on it before she came, trust that her ass was off limits even though one of the other women was fingering the other's asshole while one of the guys feasted on her pussy.

There was a certain kind of power to letting go like that. To just closing their eyes and letting the pleasure take over, carrying them away until they were in that dark, hazy place between just out of reach and oh God yes, right there.

It was that push and pull, that trust, that had lured me to rooms like this before. Yeah, I'd been in sex clubs before. None this fancy though..

The men started off with one mission. To get off as fast and as often as possible. It always happened that way. But then somewhere around the girl on girl action or sometimes a two-mouthed blow job, things changed. It became about feminine pleasure. About pleasing the women because they knew that's where they'd find all the true passion, the true ecstasy.

Right in that moment I couldn't look away, couldn't remove my hand from my slick pussy as two men feasted on a curvy redhead's pussy. Two tongues worked together, not giving a damn if they touched, hell they were practically making out on top of her clit, and the woman arched her back, writhed and gripped two thick heads of hair as she screamed her pleasure. God, it was so fucking hot my fingers were drenched with my own fucking juices.

Another woman was on her knees accepting a long thick cock like a submissive little bitch. It wasn't totally my thing but watching her close her eyes and keep her hands at her side while a man with eight pack abs and what had to be a nine inch cock slowly fucked her throat like it was a pussy.

"Oh, yes!" My words slipped out but luckily all the other in-room voyeurs were as focused on the action as I was, and I was keenly aware of a hot DILF beside me stroking his cock like it was his favorite toy. In another time and place I might have taken care of that big boner of his, but today I just wanted to watch.

Again.

I needed to be careful, coming here early could get me in a lot of trouble. Especially if I got caught by the boss, which would be bad. Very, very bad. It was bad enough the man had found his way into my shower fantasies, into my late night fantasies, hell even to my getting fucked on top of the bar fantasies. Every last fucking fantasy.

Not this one. I was determined to come without thinking about Joplin, or Saint, whatever his name was. It wouldn't be on my lips when I came this time. No. I watched the redhead squirt so hard she nearly passed out, and I rubbed three furious fingers over my clit until my own toes began to curl. The blonde getting deepthroated moaned and squeezed a guy's ass cheeks until he fucked her harder while the other girl ate her pussy as the final guy slid in and out of her pussy in a slow, drunken glide. It was hot as fuck. It was perfect. It was more than enough for me to come all over my fingers, soaking my panties and my thighs.

A tiny gasp escaped me as the last convulsion rocketed through me, and I leaned against the wall, sliding a glance to the man and woman jacking each other off beside me.

"I'd kill for a taste of that," a deep, raspy voice said to my left and I smiled at the DILF with the big cock, holding my fingers just out of his reach.

"Of this?"

He nodded, and I slicked one finger across his bottom lip.

"Yeah, that," he growled and I swear my clit vibrated against my soaked panties, sending another round of aftershocks through my body as I added another finger to his top lip this time.

"Fuck. Yeah." My hand fell away and his head fell back as long streams of jizz darted across his legs.

So. Fucking. Hot.

"Thanks for the show."

"Thanks for the taste, sweetheart." He winked and turned back to the action in the room, and I slipped out the discreet door behind a black screen on shaky legs. And I ran right into the man I was trying hard not to think about.

"Joplin," I stammered out.

"Saint," he growled. "Call me Saint."

"Saint. Hey."

"Hey yourself. Shift starts in thirty-three minutes."

"I'll be there in ten," I told him confidently. The panties were destined for the trash bin, which meant all I needed was a quick rinse of my hands and a new coat of lipstick.

"See you soon, Boss." I walked away before I said or did anything else, but the sound of his frustrated growl behind me had me wet all over again.

Maybe I'd take fifteen…just to take the edge off.

A little.

Chapter Seven

Saint

What the fuck did I just see? That was the problem with not sleeping. After a while I'd get delirious and sometimes couldn't tell fantasy from reality. Like now, I couldn't be sure that the woman I just witnessed boinking herself while watching a seven person orgy was Hazel. My fucking employee. I had to blink six, seven times just to clear all other thoughts and images from my mind. Considering her appearance in my dreams, this fucking vision could be a sign that it had finally happened.

I finally lost my fucking mind.

She'd been all alone even surrounded by other voyeurs; those dark eyes never left the action on the elevated platform as she brought herself to orgasm. Eyes squeezed tight and head tossed back with a little gasp of pleasure on her slightly parted lips, she was a magnificent sight. And it was that magnificence I couldn't get out of my head right now, while I was walking Hazel through the ins and outs of her job.

I couldn't focus because all I could see was Hazel. Only this time she was totally naked, dusty pink nipples hard and aching, as she begged me to fuck her. Begged me to take her pussy and her mouth at the same time, which seemed impossible until I looked up and saw a man with my face teasing her lips with his already hard, already leaking cock.

"Fill me up," she purred and I felt pre-come gather at the tip of my cock, making things wet behind my zipper.

"Do I leave to restock the bar myself or find someone else to do it?" Hazel looked up at me expectantly with an expression in her eyes that said it wasn't the first time she asked the question.

I had to blink to clear away the images of her naked and arching into my cock. Another round of blinking and finally the creamy swell of flesh I was seeing was Hazel's cleavage. Her mostly covered but still mouthwatering cleavage.

"Uh, we have barbacks. They will restock anything you need and keep the place clean. Some nights you'll bartend, and some nights you'll be a barback. We like to rotate the bartenders so they learn all aspects of the job. We always want to have someone at the bar. Always."

Was that tiny leather fabric even a skirt? It was so small if she sneezed I'd get a clear view of her pussy and that thought only made me wonder if she was totally bare or did she have one of those landing strips? Maybe she went old school with slick lips and a bush. "Everything you'll need, except beer, is in here." I opened the door to the stock room and motioned her inside.

If she had any hesitation about being in a small, enclosed space with me after what I'd seen her doing earlier, it didn't show on her face or her body language.

"Good to see you didn't want the stock room too close to the bar," she joked. "At least I'll get some killer guns from this job."

How could she stand there and joke about muscles and lemon slices when I caught her, my employee, fingering herself right before work?

"Yeah," I grunted, sounding a lot like our resident grumpy asshole, Gunnar.

Her smile slipped just a little but I could see in those big brown eyes that she wanted to talk. About something and I had a damn good clue what.

"Listen, Saint, we should—"

"No. We shouldn't. There's no need to talk about anything."

All of a sudden I was acting like a pearl-clutching prude and that pissed me off. I was a goddamn soldier, made of tougher stuff than a sexy masturbating woman.

Hazel laughed at me for a moment before her expression sobered and she crowded my space. How the hell someone so small could invade my space and make me feel trapped, I had no goddamn clue, but the little pixie managed it.

"I'm Hazel and I like orgies," she blurted out. "Actually I like all manner of fucked up fucking, mostly watching, but occasionally joining in because it helps me relax and deal with my shit. Problems or questions?"

Her tough girl attitude and direct words made me like her even more, goddammit. A reluctant smile spread across my face because the only question I wanted to ask—*how often and can I join in?* But it was highly fucking inappropriate.

"Your sex life is your business, Hazel. Not mine." Even though parts of me wanted to make it my business. Right here in this dark, cramped room.

"It is my business," she agreed, crossing her arms once again over her chest without realizing just how mouthwatering it made her tits look. Soft creamy swells of flesh pushed up and out, making it hard to look at anything else, though her miles of legs were a tempting sight on their own.

"But I'm not ashamed, so if you want to say something speak now or forever hold your peace."

"Forever?" I quirked a questioning brow at her, feeling humor tugging at my mouth.

"Forever," she confirmed and took another step closer until hard peaks brushed against my chest. Hazel stepped back and I took the opportunity to make my escape, reaching behind me for the knob only the damn thing cracked me in the base of my spine.

"Shit!" The next few seconds unfolded in slow motion. I fell forward with Hazel right in my path and reached out to grab her, my hands somehow finding her slender waist as I continued to stumble forward until she was smashed between me and a shelf filled with napkins, towels and buckets of cocktail garnishes.

"Fuck, I'm sorry."

"No worries." Her words came out breathless and warm against my skin, big brown eyes flecked with flakes of green stared up at me, dilated and full of desire. Her pulse raced at the base of her throat and her tongue slicked across full, red painted lips. Those damn nipples, hard enough to cut glass, dug into my ribs with every shallow breath she took.

My cock was hard as steel and pressed against her thigh and any hope I had that she hadn't noticed, died with that self-satisfied smirk she wore.

"Sorry about that."

Her smile widened and Hazel, the tease, licked her lips once again.

"Don't be. I'll be at the bar," she said and walked away with, I swear, an extra swing in her step.

When Hazel was out of sight, I went in search of a private spot to relieve the ache in my cock.

Chapter Eight

Hazel

Holy shit. I just had a moment. With my boss. An honest to goodness, hot as fuck, wet my panties and make me think about letting him tie me up and fuck me until I squirted all over the place, moment. *Shit.*

It was hot as fuck and now I couldn't stop thinking about it because it proved one thing. I hadn't been sure when I started this job, if Saint was more of a sinner than he pretended to be. Up close, he was hotter and more masculine than meek. Strong. Dark. Intense. He was a walking, talking temptation and that just wouldn't do.

Saint was my boss and mixing business with pleasure was a recipe for disaster. Girls like me always lost out when sexy times happened at the office. Right now I needed this job more than I needed a good hard fuck. Which was too bad, because after the show in the room before work, I really needed a good hard fuck.

Unfortunately, this job garnered hundreds of dollars of tips for nothing more than smiling while showing skin and whipping up overpriced cocktails.

God bless Texas!

Fucking, however, did *not* garner such tips.

Maybe it did, but times weren't that hard. *Yet.*

Dammit!

***

The super sexy moment with Saint had kept me good and horny for days. Days upon days, which made my shifts at The Barn Door long and painful. Agonizing, even. I'd spent the past few days staying out of his way and making sure he stayed as far away from me as possible. Being stuck at a twelve-foot-long bar, wasn't anyone's definition of space and every night I'd spend a good hour with my vibrator. Moaning and thrashing over images of my boss and coming until I was too tired to do anything but drift off to sleep.

Rinse and repeat. All night, he riled me up without doing or saying anything, just his look and his scent.

Fuck! And that dark stare that saw everything but said nothing. Today though, I was determined to change things. To swing the odds in my favor.

I knew from those lingering looks that Saint wanted me. He might not want to want me, but he did. His eyes didn't lie and neither did the bulge in his fucking pants, and that was what gave me hope. Not in a realistic way, of course. I was far too cynical to have any actual hope, but those looks gave me just enough hope to leave my panties at home when I left for today's shift.

That was what this was all about. Saint had some kind of invisible pull, invisible control over my body, and I needed to overcome it. To power through it so things could get back to normal. So I skipped going to the club on my last night off, opting for another night with a vibrator and my favorite porn stars because there was no fucking way I'd get off to images of Saint.

Again.

I took a deep breath and smoothed damp hands over my postage stamp denim skirt and stepped inside the club. Tonight was amateur night, and Gunnar had asked me to dress the part. I went above and beyond in a white lace tank that made my tits look divine, red cowboy boots to match my lips and two dark braids peeking from underneath a Stetson. I was a cowboy's wet dream, which I hoped translated into big ass tips for me tonight.

"You're late," Saint's voice growled behind me, startling me.

I refused to show it, tightening my shoulders before glancing over one to look at him. Big mistake because tonight he wore the male equivalent of my own outfit, only he filled out that white t-shirt so fucking deliciously, I had a sharp reminder of my panty-less state. "I'm fifteen minutes early, actually."

He growled again and my nipples responded. Instantly. "You're on the front bar. Again."

"Got it," I told him, my voice a little too bright as I stomped off to the employee locker room where my keys and bag would be safe during my shift. I tried not to let his shitty attitude get to me, but it was hard not to take it personally, even with all the hot as fuck looks he sent my way. Saint didn't like me. I had no clue why, but something about me turned his smile into a scowl, and his happy mood darkened when I came around.

It was enough to give a girl a complex.

If I was an ordinary girl, it might have. But I wasn't, I recognized the pain I saw in Saint's beautiful green eyes, and I saw right through his cool business demeanor he used to hide the pain. I recognized the hint of darkness I saw in him, the darkness that terrified him because he didn't know how to embrace it. Not yet.

I had to laugh at myself. Hint of darkness. What the fuck did that even mean? It meant that my one and only friend Jessie, with her romantic tendencies and love of all things lovey-dovey, was rubbing off on me. She was a die-hard romantic, and I knew she'd see some hero worthy of saving when she saw Saint, instead of a flashing neon sign with the word DANGER staring back, like I did.

Jessie had her own happy ending so she saw love everywhere, but she was the outlier. The anomaly. People like Saint and me didn't get what she had, so she wasn't able to see things clearly. I could, though. So I knew there was no point in seeing any more than what Saint presented to the world. It was what he wanted the world to see, which meant that was who he wanted to be.

And that was just perfect for me. It would allow me to have a little fun while seeking a bit of revenge for him being a dick. By the end of my shift, we'd see just how much of a *saint* he really was.

Chapter Nine

Saint

"Oh, excuse me." Hazel's voice was husky and innocent. Too goddamn innocent considering it was the fiftieth time she'd accidentally bumped or rubbed up against me.

"Don't worry about it," I grunted, but the truth was she was a sexual harassment lawsuit waiting to happen. The worst part was that I couldn't be sure she did it on purpose because two people squeezed into a twelve foot by five-foot space meant things were pretty cramped behind the bar, so I couldn't outright accuse her. No matter how hard it was to ignore. I needed to escape, even if it was just temporarily. "I'll be back."

"I'll be right here," she said in a sing-song voice that hit me right between the legs.

The woman was too much temptation and the worst part of it was that she didn't have a fucking clue. At least I hoped she didn't, because that was the only thing keeping me from taking her hard and fast in a dark corner of the club.

"Saint, there you are. How's it going man?" Gunnar wore a wide smile that I knew meant he'd just been with his woman. Or was on his way to see her. Either way, he was happy.

"Good. Just came to grab some more napkins." It was as good a lie as any and the supply closet was only a few feet away.

"Full already? You think it's because of amateur night?"

I nodded at his enthusiastic question. When I'd first met Gunnar, I wasn't sure if he ever smiled, but the more he whipped Hardtail Ranch into shape, the more he smiled. Laughed. Joked, even. It was a little disturbing, but I was also happy for anyone who managed to say *fuck off* to their demons.

"Safe to say that's why. The crowd is huge."

"Good," he said, but then his brows rose. "We have about a dozen new members coming in tonight, all under thirty and most of them men. Keep an eye on the front bar tonight. And Hazel."

"She's a big girl, Gunnar. And we have security." I couldn't tell if he was attracted to her or wary of Hazel, but his interest in her was odd.

"She is, and she's also a damn good bartender, not to mention one of my employees. I just want to make sure she feels as safe as she actually is."

Ah hell, now I couldn't stop thinking about hands grabbing and tugging on her against her will. Brown eyes wide and terrified, searching for a helping hand and not finding one. Fuck. "You can count on me, Gunnar."

"I know I can." He smiled again and gave my back a playful slap. Then his expression sobered. "Big Mac's place got robbed last night."

Those were the last damn words I expected to hear. Big Mac was a good guy, a good man, and I knew enough bad ones to know the difference. The tall man with the ginger beard had a smile for everyone, never forgot a name, and would order whatever you needed without judgment or questions. "Is he all right?"

Gunnar nodded but I knew he was downplaying it. "Mac's a bit banged up and one eye is swollen shut but he's fine. Ready to light a fire up under someone's ass."

Not that I blamed him. Opey was his hometown, born and raised and Mac was proud of the fact that Opey had one of the lowest crime rates in all of Texas. These robberies had probably pissed him off good and then for him to get hit, he was probably on a rampage. I knew what needed to be done and no matter how unsure I felt about it, I knew it was the right thing. "Recon tonight?"

A small smile pulled across Gunnar's lips. "Tonight. After closing." Gunnar held out his hand and I took it, shaking it the way men like us did. Firm and brief. "We won't do anything we don't need to. I promise."

I believed him. "Tonight, then." I knew Gunnar wouldn't lead any of us into a situation we couldn't get out of so I pushed my negative thoughts away for now and headed back to the bar. With napkins.

Hazel wore a bright smile for two couples, one older and the other much younger, while whipping up some kind of fancy cocktail.

"Then we add the egg white. Sounds weird, I know but it's what makes all the difference. If you've ever had it the right way, you'll never be able to have it any other way." She gave the shaker a good shake, tits jiggling tantalizingly beneath white lace. All four sets of eyes were glued to the movement, the press of her nipples against the lace, slowly hardening as she poured the drinks.

"Cheers!" Her smile was wide and her eyes shiny with happiness, but it all rang a little hollow.

Everyone took a sip and declared her a genius before walking away. The older woman walked back with desire in her eyes and slid a hundred dollar bill towards Hazel.

"I hope to see you in one of the rooms sometime soon." She winked and walked away.

Surprisingly, Hazel gave her one short look and went back to work, not bothered by the blatant desire of the other woman. I wondered if she was considering it, if she would find one or both of those couples another time and let them have their way with her. Did that kind of thing really do it for her?

Shit, who was I to judge? I hadn't been with a woman since, hell since Iceland. Maybe I needed some kinky shit to bring me back to life. She did say she used it to relax. Maybe it would work for me? Then again, maybe not.

"You handled that well," I told her when I was close enough to feel the heat coming off her body.

She shrugged. "They were nice people so what's the point in being rude? Besides, you never know what the future might hold."

I wanted to know more about that but a rush of people came to the bar all at once, forcing Hazel and I to work very closely and very quickly. I spent the next few hours with a permanent hardon where that sweet little ass brushed across my zipper at least a hundred times. Did the woman not believe in wearing a bra? Every time she scooted past me; her hard nipples scraped against my chest. Sometimes a hand would slide across my midsection or over my ass. It was torture.

Pure fucking torture. She smelled like sex and candy. Intoxicating and irresistible.

"Comin' through!" she said.

Before I could move, Hazel was sidestepping past me with four glasses in her hands and her ass giving me the biggest goddamn boner of the night.

"Shit," I bit out and went the opposite way, sticking close to the bar while I got a few whiskeys for a couple of the older members. "There ya go," I said as I served them, brighter than I felt.

Finally, the crowd thinned as couples, triples and singles danced and mingled, flirted and sized up the others in the room, searching for who would help them fulfill tonight's fantasies. It was always like that at the start of a shift and in an hour, maybe eighty-five minutes, they would all be back, sated and thirsty and ready for round two. With all the amateurs in the house tonight, it could get even crazier.

"Got it!" Hazel's shout of distress drew my attention and I was right behind her as she leaned over the bar to catch a falling cocktail glass. Long, shapely legs dangled in the air but then something else, a flash of pink, caught my eye.

Not just pink. Bare, pink lips. Puffy pink pussy lips stared back at me far too fucking briefly, but long enough to make my mouth water and my cock harden. I grabbed her by the waist and pulled her back with a grunt. "Careful."

"Thanks," she said on a breathy sigh, big brown eyes shining up at me with gratitude.

I held her close for another minute, bending to her ear.

"I'll be back." I needed a dark corner or a cold fucking shower.

Maybe it was time to find a hot, willing woman. One who didn't work for me.

How hard could that be? I was in a fucking sex club.

KB Winters

Chapter Ten

Hazel

"Finally!" At The Barn Door, there was closing time and then there was time to go home time. Closing time happened an hour after last call because Gunnar wanted to give the members time to get themselves together so they went out into the streets of conservative west Texas with their hair and clothes all proper like, at least that was how Holden had put it. Now that the last members were out the door, Saint locked it behind them and we got busy with the work the customers didn't get to see.

Luckily, it wasn't part of my job to clean bodily fluids, sex toys and other equipment, so I gingerly stepped over discarded items as I grabbed all the leftover glasses. As usual, there were glasses everywhere and it took almost an hour just to gather them all, stack them and take them to the dishwasher in the kitchen. Next up I had to clean the tables in the bar. Each and every damn one.

It was a boring job whose only real fault was that it was tedious, but I had five hundred bucks worth of tips in my pocket so none of the after shift jobs got to me.

Or maybe it was the arousal coursing through my body, the same way it had been all night. Working in a sex club turned me on seven ways to Sunday but doing it alongside Saint was torture on the lady bits. Actually painful.

I didn't know why in the hell I thought I could fuck with a guy like Saint and leave completely unaffected, because I couldn't. It was just impossible. Brushing up against him and the sculpted muscles of his chest, abs and, yes, Lord, even his ass, had been my undoing. I was wet and swollen and the only recourse on tap was my hand or my toys, neither of which I was hungry for at the moment. No, there was just one man that would satisfy my appetite and I couldn't have him.

Not if I wanted to keep my job.

"At least the tables are done," I muttered to myself and tossed the last few towels into the laundry bin that would get picked up tomorrow. Then I headed downstairs to the employee locker room to change my shirt and grab my bag. I wouldn't go searching for Saint until I was ready to walk out the door. I needed distance if there was even a glimmer of a chance that I wouldn't do something stupid.

The last time I did something stupid, I lived to regret it. Twice. Nope, this time I'd be smart. Reasonable. And like a smart, reasonable employee, I changed my shirt and grabbed my bag, but the sound of the shower spray around the corner called to me like a siren's song and I peeked to see who was still here.

Except it wasn't a siren, it was something better. Much, much better. It was Saint, naked as the day he was born with soap and water highlighting all the dips and planes of his gorgeous body. His skin was smooth minus a few scars and knife wounds, which didn't hold my attention as much as it brought to the surface just how real his pain was. The tattoos, they held my attention. Tribal tattoos covered his chest and arms, and a long script down the right side of his waist. God they were everywhere. Beautiful. Badass.

He was a sight to behold, all wet with rippling muscles that helped him move with the grace of a dancer. And the fact that he didn't see me yet only made me look harder, memorize more details. Lick my lips at the sight of his cock, long though it was completely flaccid.

"Hazel, what the fuck?"

God, that little twitch of his cock did more for me in that moment than the angry scowl on his face and I stared just a little bit longer before I licked my lips again.

"I just came to tell you that I'm headed out." The words came out just as I intended, only my feet didn't move. Wouldn't move. Couldn't.

He put the towel to his face to wipe away the water, giving me time to move forward as the devil took hold of my body. "Maybe you should g—"

WICKED

I didn't let Saint finish his words because I didn't want to hear them, all I wanted in that moment was him. Just a little taste of him because I wasn't ready for more with anyone and certainly not him.

"—Maybe I should," I told him with a smile as my hand wrapped around his semi-hard cock and squeezed. "Do you want me to leave, Saint?" I stroked his cock long and slow until it was thick and hard, stealing from him his ability to speak.

His only response was a grunt as I took his towel and dropped it between us before I fell to my knees. Up close, his cock was a thing of beauty, long without a doubt, but thick enough that he'd be a challenge to take deep. The big vein on the underside throbbed when I licked it and his knees trembled when I flicked my tongue over the spot at the back of his sac.

"Hazel." That was it, just my name, like it was the only thing he could say as passion overtook him.

I closed my eyes and wrapped my lips around the head of his dick, enjoying the way he couldn't stop moaning and groaning and growling as I licked him. I tasted every inch of Saint, keeping my eyes closed as I licked him from the underside of his balls to the slit on the head.

"Oh, fuck. Hazel, fuck."

I smiled at the strained passion in his voice and took him deeper, savoring the flavor of pre-come as it burst on my tongue. My lips slid down the length of him and my tongue joined in, giving him the kind of slick friction that made a man forget he was a gentleman. His hips started to buck and I relaxed, opened myself up to him as heat spread through my body. He went deeper as his hips began to buck on their own free will.

Then he froze. "Shit," he groaned and pulled back, looking apologetic as fuck.

"No. Don't stop. I like it." It was true and I sat there, waiting for him to judge me. For disgust to settle on his face, but it didn't. His green-eyed gaze seared through me, trying to see my soul to make sure this was what I wanted, and I let him look because I fucking wanted it. All of it. Bad.

"Fuck, Hazel." Saint gripped his cock, finally on board with the plan, stroking it as he looked at me and pressed his tip to my lips. "Take it."

My mouth opened instantly and he slid in and then out. In again and then out. He kept a slow and steady pace that was like adding one hay straw at a time to the fire, but it was so fucking hot. He moved faster and faster, fucking my mouth and then my throat like he owned it, like it was his to punish and pleasure as he saw fit.

I couldn't look away from him, sliding his cock in and out of my mouth, deeper and deeper still until he hit the back of my throat, fucking me until my eyes watered. And they watered but they never left him, not his beautiful face contorted in erotic pain and not his spectacular body in action. He was so fucking hot I was getting turned on all over again just watching him have his way with my mouth.

"Hazel," he groaned and his hips sped up, telling me what my tongue could already feel. His cock growing impossibly harder as his balls drew up tight in preparation for his release.

"Oh fuck," he growled as he pumped his cock and splashed into my face, my hair, my mouth—hot and salty and plentiful. "Shit!"

I smiled around his cock, sucking the tip until I knew every drop was gone. Until his legs buckled and his hands flew out to the tile wall to keep him upright. I stood and straightened my skirt and hair, as I licked my lips. "You're every bit as good as I thought you would be. Good night, Saint."

He choked out an unintelligible response and cocked his head, like he was trying to figure me out. "Good uhm, night."

I went over to the sink and stared in the mirror. I had Saint's come all over my face, neck and hair. It looked hot. As fuck. I pulled out my phone and snapped a mirror selfie before he finished drying off. This would be good for my spank bank. My sexy boss, Saint's come all over me.

WICKED

I chuckled to myself as I rinsed my face and hands.

It had been a damn good night. I had a ton of money in my pocket and the taste of a hot man on my tongue. I was headed home to finish what he'd started.

I smiled again and begged my legs to move faster to get away from Saint, just in case he had the crazy thought that he needed to return the favor. I wasn't ready for that. Not yet.

Maybe not ever.

KB Winters

Chapter Eleven

Saint

I watched Hazel spin on her heels and flounce the fuck out of the locker room, leaving me stunned with a fading erection. I couldn't believe what the fuck had just happened. Did Hazel, my employee, creep into the shower to watch me and the suck me off—hard—until I damn near fell to my knees thanks to a wicked orgasm? I didn't know what her game was but it had to be a game because I met plenty of women in my life, many of them down to fuck without any other promises, but a free, no strings attached blow job? That shit was un-fucking-heard of.

But she'd done it. I never imagined her full lips wrapped around my cock, taking me deep until I hit the back of her throat, and I knew for a damn fact that I didn't imagine the way she sucked me dry. She didn't even cringe when I came on her face. It was a helluva blow job, one I wouldn't soon forget either.

Just because I wouldn't forget the way she gave head; didn't mean I'd give Hazel whatever it was she was after. Chances were good that I didn't even have it to give and if I did, I wouldn't.

Couldn't.

She'd show her true colors soon enough, and I planned to give her enough distance to do just that. In the meantime, I needed another goddamn shower, this time ice cold with as much pressure as the spray would allow. The cold water felt good, if jarring, on my overheated skin, and I stood there with my eyes closed and my hands braced on the wall as I tried to wash away the images of my cock in Hazel's mouth running through my mind.

Images of how she'd been just minutes ago, on her knees with fire burning in those deep coffee brown eyes as she sucked me off. Took me willingly and with an energy few women had ever shown when it came to the art of sucking a dick properly. It made me wonder what else she liked, besides sucking dick and getting off watching orgies.

My hand wrapped around my cock, already hard again from replaying the blow job, and I wondered what else she'd like. Would she like it if I wrapped my hands around her delicate throat and squeezed while I plowed into her as hard and fast as I could, sweat dripping from my body onto hers as she gasped for breath while her pussy clamped down tight around me. Would it get her off? Make her even wetter until only the slick sounds of our fucking tore through the air?

Another thought occurred and I strangled my cock hard, pumping with more force than necessary as I thought about bending her over until that heart shaped ass was in the air, wiggling anxiously as my tongue closed in on that tight asshole. I wondered if she would welcome this cock in her asshole, would she push back and beg for more? Or would she require some coaxing? Would she respond to sweet words or promises of endless ecstasy?

"Fuck!" I pumped my cock faster.

She was definitely a woman motivated by pleasure, and I dreamed of giving it to her in all kinds of ways. In every position imaginable, I wanted her. Wanted to fuck all her holes, maybe all at once with a dildo or vibrator.

"Oh fuck!" Another cry shot out of me as I wondered if she would let me fuck her throat with a rubber cock or did she only respond that way to the real thing? Would she choke and gag the same or would she ask me to take her while I fucked her ass with a toy?

My orgasm shot out of me like a rocket, long streams of come hitting the slick shower walls before sliding down, vanishing down the drain like it never even happened.

But it had happened and even though I was all cleaned up and all traces of my pleasure were gone, I couldn't forget it.

Not ever.

Closing up the bar took a few more minutes and then I was headed back to the bunkhouse. Where for once, I slept like a goddamn baby.

Chapter Twelve

Hazel

Another long day and another long shift, but still I walked out of The Barn Door with a bounce in my step because my jean pockets were full to overflowing with tips. Hundreds of dollars worth of tips should have weighed me down, but I walked through the parking lot as light as I'd ever felt. This might have been what normal felt like. The people who woke up each morning happy with the world, kissing their loved ones before they headed out for a productive day at the office, but not just productive—happily productive. It was an important distinction, one that not many people understood but one that people like me couldn't afford to forget.

My tips allowed me to squirrel away a shit ton of money for a rainy day because one thing I'd learned about life, was that rain was inevitable. This time though, I wouldn't be caught unprepared. The way I was on my eighteenth birthday and my foster family had woken me up with a delightful surprise. Silly, naïve little girl that I was, had been expecting a birthday cake and maybe some small trinket to commemorate becoming an adult. What I got instead was a navy blue backpack filled with my shit and a half-hearted wave that said, 'don't let the door hit ya on the way out.'

It had taken another hard won lesson, in the form of a no good boyfriend before the lesson had stuck, but it had. Thankfully.

I slid behind the wheel of my beat up old car, smiling at the full tank of gas and the no longer flashing check engine light. It felt good to be back on my feet again, even if the rest of my world was up in the air.

The familiar tone ringing from my phone had a smile on my lips as I answered. "Jessie! How the hell are you, girl?" Jessie was my bestie, when she had time to be. Hell, she was the only person in the world who gave a damn about me.

Her sweet laughter put me at ease, confirming that she was still as happy as she was when I'd seen her last summer. "I'm good, missing my girl. How are things in good ol' Texas, Hazel?"

I closed my eyes and just listened to the sound of her voice for a few moments. It was a familiar sound, even and sweet and slightly melodic. I missed that sound like crazy. "Texas is...good. Weird. But I got a great job and the tips are amazing."

Jessie whooped, a loud sound that made me smile as I shifted the car into drive and began the short trip home. "Who would have thought two foster kids from Arkansas would end up doing so well?"

Her words were kind, but the truth was that Jessie had gone out and grabbed life by the balls, reaching out for the life she wanted. And she'd gotten it. Spectacularly.

"Well, you have three beautiful kids and a husband who thinks you are a walking, talking goddess, so yeah, you are doing well. Really well. I work at a sex club and live in an apartment that's a half step up from a roach motel."

"Wow. You are moving up. Sex club, huh? How fun!"

"God, Jessie, if you only knew what perverted rich people did. It's crazy."

"And that's still more than what you started out with, girl. Be proud of what you do! You have a job that allows you to take care of yourself, a car to get you wherever you want to go without asking anyone's permission, and a place to lay your head at night. How many times did we wish for something so simple?"

"Too many times," I told her on a sigh. There had been many nights where we went to bed hungry, wishing for adulthood when we didn't have to rely on anyone else. "How's your cowboy?"

"Great," she cooed. "Jake signed a contract with the biggest seller of organic beef which means we can stop worrying about money so much."

"Wow, that's great Jess. Congratulations!" Not having to worry about money was a dream that no foster kid was ever dumb enough to hope for, but somehow Jessie had gotten it for her and her family. "So you're a real cowgirl now, selling beef and everything."

Her laugh trilled down the line making me smile. "Complete with muddy jeans, sun weathered skin and hair that could use a deep conditioning, if only I had the time."

"Luckily, Jake loves you with freckles and split ends." I'd only met Jake a handful of times, but he was a good man with a big heart, and he got bonus points because he didn't mind our close relationship.

"He's pretty great," she said, and I knew she was smiling because I could hear it in her voice. "Speaking of, tell me about all that gorgeous hunks you work with and don't even try to downplay it," she threatened.

Jessie was the one person I didn't have to hide from, so even though I didn't want to talk about it, I told her about The Barn Door. I told her about Gunnar and the rest of the guys, and of course I told her all about Saint as I shoved my key in the door and locked myself inside my hovel, er, apartment. "They're all nice guys, most of them are veterans."

"Oh wow," she sighed softly. "Which one do you like?"

"Who said I liked any of them? They're all nice guys, Jessie."

"I'm calling bullshit and if my best friend radar is accurate, you have a thing for the one called Saint."

"Sometimes I hate that you know me so well." It was the one downside to having a best friend forever. She knew me well and remembered everything.

"I remember saying the same thing when someone stopped me from running away, while pregnant, from a man who loved me. So what aren't you telling me?"

There was no point in dragging it out, especially now that I had a big glass of cheap wine at my side. "There's been this weird tension between me and Saint, sexual and dark and hot. He barely even likes me, for some reason, but he wants me."

"And you want him," she said confidently.

"Yeah. And something sort of happened." I didn't want to tell her. Not because Jessie judged, but because she gave a damn. I closed my eyes and told her about what happened in the shower.

Jessie sighed and I could hear the disapproval in her voice. "I thought you weren't gonna do that anymore, Hazel. Did he force you?"

Yeah, I had made that promise, but I thought she realized at the time I was lying. "No! He looked so tasty all naked and wet, fresh from the shower. I couldn't resist."

My clit swelled and ached at the memory, and I had to cross my legs until the sensation passed.

"Hazel, if you're not ready to give a man all of you, then he doesn't deserve any of you. Dammit, give yourself a chance to be happy."

And that was exactly why I loved her, because my sister of the heart believed I deserved more than the string of shitty boyfriends and mediocre lays I've had in my life.

"I am happy, Jessie. Just not the kind of happy you have going on over there in Oklahoma." I didn't want to make her feel bad, but I needed her to understand. "Not everyone gets that kind of happy and that's okay. I have a job and I can take care of myself. That's happiness for me. And as much as I want to, and believe me I do, I can't sleep with my boss. Not again."

"You didn't sleep with him, Hazel, that bastard sexually assaulted you!"

She was getting riled up again, and I knew I needed to calm her down before she had a panic attack, or worse. My old boss was in prison now, and if this didn't stop she'd try to get to the bastard. Jessie was a sweetheart but she could be psycho when someone threatened those she loved.

"He tried to, Jessie, but he failed. That's what's important." I hated even thinking about that asshole, that shitty job I'd stayed in because I needed a place to live. My boss had known it and the moment opportunity struck; he went for it. Promising me a raise and then holding me down while he finger fucked me. The fucking creep. Touching my pussy like I belonged to him. Like he fucking owned me.

"Girl don't do things that you don't have to do. Not if you don't want to."

"But that's the difference! I *did* want to, Jessie. Saint is so fucking gorgeous and the fact that he doesn't even like me, helps."

"Exactly!" Jessie growled. "Don't give up your goodies to a man who doesn't appreciate you, dammit. You're great and wonderful, so smart and generous and kind, and these assholes don't deserve you!"

There was a long pause before I spoke again. "You done, Reverend?"

Jessie burst out laughing and in the background, her youngest, Riley, let out a frustrated cry. "Yeah, I'm done. I'm serious though, Hazel. Promise that you'll value yourself at least as much as I do."

"I promise to try. How's that?"

"Acceptable. For now." There was a long pause and some cooing in the background as she settled Riley. "In the meantime, you can start setting aside a week or two to come for a visit. Shannon can't wait to share all the girly shit you send her, and Lord knows I'm tired of sitting for makeup sessions and pretend hair salon."

Her oldest daughter was a spitfire, destined to be a troublemaker just like her favorite aunt.

"I'll see what I can swing, but I just started so it might be some time before I'm even eligible for paid time off."

I didn't want to rock the boat just yet, at least not until I replenished my savings enough that losing the job wouldn't matter. Wouldn't hurt. That was how the game was played. I got a new job and gave it my all, doing the tasks that were asked of me without giving anyone any shit. Unless it was warranted. Then when I got enough money saved, I still did my job, only then I began to tally up all the grievances and mistreatments until I couldn't take it anymore, or until I got fired.

Whichever came first.

"I miss you, Hazel. Next time you move, come back to Oklahoma."

It was an old argument. One I had no desire to rehash. "I'll keep it on the list of options, but you know how I feel about repeats." I didn't stay in the same place twice, and I didn't go back to old lovers or friends with benefits. It was a rule that kept me from becoming to fanciful, to wishful.

"Yeah but I was hoping that rule wouldn't apply to your only family." There was that guilt that only family could heap upon me. And Jessie was the only family I had, but thankfully I only had to deal with her in small doses on our monthly talks. We connected more if we needed to.

Lately, Jessie hadn't needed it much so I tried not to need her as much either. "I'll come visit as soon as I can."

"Fine, I accept that answer. Now. Just, next time something happens with this Saint character, make sure you get his mouth in return. Get a little bit of heat for you too."

My mouth opened, and I actually blushed. Then I closed it, speechless.

After a few seconds, she asked, "You still there?"

"I'm still here, and I'll take it under consideration. I promise."

"Good because I have to go. The savages need attention," she said as the background noise grew louder.

"All right. Give everyone a hug and a kiss for me, and I'll talk to you soon. Love you." It was always hard to say goodbye to Jessie, had been since I'd left her in Oklahoma years ago with Jake. Every time we said it, a little piece of my heart broke just a little more.

"Love you more, girl. Bye." The call ended and as usual, I felt lighter. Freer. More like the woman I should have been, could have been, if my life had turned out differently.

I missed Jessie like crazy, but I also envied her and what she had. Not that I wanted Jake or her loveable, energy-sucking ankle biters, but the love she had, the life she had. I craved a life like that, more so with every passing year.

Which made it hard to see it all up close and in living color. But I would visit, as soon as I could. As soon as I was ready.

In the meantime, I wished for Jessie's optimism. Saint was too fucked up for anything normal. I knew that much even if I didn't have all the details and wasn't sure what the hell a normal relationship looked like. But his brand of fucked up could likely be healed. He was a soldier after all, but there was a good chance that he was too normal for the type of fucked up that seemed to follow me wherever I went.

It was a nice thought, though, that Saint and I could have some normal relationship like Jessie and Jake, but it was just that. A thought.

A fantasy that, like so many others, would soon be forgotten the moment Saint revealed himself to be no different from any other man I'd ever come across.

For now, he would remain a sexual fantasy that I used to get me through the hard times, because in my life, the hard times were always more plentiful than the good ones.

Chapter Thirteen

Saint

"We could've taken the bikes tonight," I told Gunnar as we left Hardtail Ranch in our rearview and headed for Opey proper. I wasn't completely comfortable on the damn thing yet, but a little bit of practice each day had helped.

"We could have, but this way we blend in, which is what we want for now." Gunnar kept his gaze on a swivel while I drove the dark two-lane highway that dropped us right in the center of Small Town, USA.

Opey wasn't just a small town, it was *the* proverbial small town, with wooden sidewalks on both sides of the main strip of commerce, colorful awnings with catchy business names like Curl of the World Beauty Salon, the Opey Doke Café and my personal favorite, Doggone Tires, where you could get wheels for everything from motorcycles and ATVs to tractors, mowers and even cars.

This time of night a lot of the smaller shops had already rolled up the streets and tucked itself in for the night. "Shit it's quiet around here. No wonder these guys strike so late at night. No one's around to hear." It wasn't a secret that I wasn't completely sold on the idea of going after these guys. But seeing Opey like this, all innocent and quiet, pissed me off, that these good, hard working people were being victimized for being, well, good hard working people.

We rounded a corner and Big Mac's place came into view.

"Son of a bitch!" The big window with a cartoon image of the man himself and the store logo emblazoned across the front had been replaced with plain old ugly ass boarded up stand-in. "That shit just ain't right."

Gunnar's deep chuckle sounded beside me, his blue eyes missing nothing as we drove through town.

"Ye Olde Stuff has already replaced its windows, at least." He nodded in the direction of the antique store with the funny name. The old stained glass windows had been replaced with replicas, but they didn't have the old world feel of the originals.

Many units were available for rent above the businesses, clearly built before people worried about things like safety hazards and fire escapes. Every block of the main strip was pretty much the same: big picture windows so proprietors might entice tourists and shoppers inside to boost the economy. But as we rounded every corner, something became clear to me.

"This is a crew. I'm sure of it."

Gunnar nodded silently as I drove down another street that connected with the final dead end street where the City Hall and Courthouse complex took up an enormous plot of land. "I think so too, but what makes you so sure?"

I looked at the Prez and wondered if he was placating the head case or if he really gave a damn what I thought. Giving him the benefit of the doubt, I sighed and slowed the car down.

"The businesses that were hit so far, they all have at least two entry points. Hell, probably only two entry points. I'll bet you anything that the doors in back have little to no security." It had been a safe town, and no one would have thought to spend the extra money on security when it had never been an issue. "I bet those fuckers broke the front windows as a distraction so they could escape out the back. It's what I would do if I was a criminal. And that's only based on a cursory glance of the layout."

A slow smile spread from Gunnar's left ear to his right as he turned to face me. "I knew you were the right fuckin' guy for this job."

I didn't believe that shit for one second, but I could see that Gunnar did and instead of wondering why, I merely shrugged. "Dude, it's one small detail," I argued.

"Maybe so, but logistics is your shit, man. You see what other people miss and if we can figure out who these motherfuckers are, then we can come up with a response. An appropriate response," he amended in deference to my reluctance for vengeance. "This is exactly why we need you, Saint. You'll keep the rest of us from going all the way off the deep end."

"Then we're all fucked," I told him as I thought about the three men who'd needed me, who'd depended on me to keep them safe, who had relied on me to make choices that wouldn't kill them. They were all dead and buried, proving once again that I wasn't up to the task.

"Peaches was right about you, Saint." I stifled the urge to tell him I didn't give a fuck what Peaches thought because the truth was, she was cool as fuck and treated us all like family. Also, disrespecting the Prez's woman seemed a good way to earn an ass whooping from the whole MC.

"Yeah, what was she right about?" Peaches hadn't lived an easy life so I was sure her insights to Gunnar were about as accurate as they'd been when she gave them to me.

"She said that you underestimate yourself and your worth. I thought it was just PTSD but I'm starting to think that, once again, she's right."

His lips quirked into a smile as I made a U-turn at the dead end, giving the other side of the street a careful look.

"Don't tell her I said that."

"Somehow I'm betting she already knows," I told him with a laugh. Hiding shit from that woman was useless, but Peaches wasn't pushy or overbearing. She knew everything it seemed and waited until you were ready to talk about it.

Gunnar nodded, a small smile still on his lips as he looked out his window. I turned to mine. Other than a few stragglers and small groups of teenagers, the town was quiet as a cemetery. Finally, Gunnar's voice broke the silence. "How are things going at The Barn Door?"

His question made me immediately suspicious, and I wondered if Hazel had said something to him. "Fine. Why do you ask?"

"Curiosity," he said with a careless shrug that put me at ease right away. He didn't know that I'd shirked my responsibilities where she was concerned, ignoring Hazel when I should have been training her all because those dark, haunted features were invading my dreams.

"I didn't think you'd say even if something was wrong or you needed more help, so I figured I'd ask." He laughed again. "Peaches swears asking is an effective mode of communication, but I ain't sold on it yet."

I laughed right along with him because I wasn't sold either.

"Maybe Peaches and Mitch have been comparing notes." I regretted those words instantly, but Gunnar let the comment hang in the air for a long time, not bothering to respond.

"It's dead tonight," he finally said with resignation. "We have to figure out how they're choosing the businesses so we can figure out who they are."

He seemed so frustrated that I began to sympathize with Gunnar, to understand a bit more about why he wanted to do this for the town. For the club.

"See if Peaches can access any security footage in town. It might lead somewhere," I said. "I suspect Big Mac had some type of security system, and I'd bet that antique shop did as well. Even small town folks cared about insurance premiums, especially where their livelihoods were concerned."

"Good idea," he said and we took off. After several circuits of the town, I aimed the car back toward the ranch. We drove for a long time in companionable silence.

"You've talked to Mitch," he said out of the blue.

"I have." It wasn't a secret, but like we'd just discussed, talking wasn't one of my favorite past times so I kept my secrets to myself. "I had a fucked up dream and figured he could help."

"What was the dream?"

I should have known he'd want details. Gunnar seemed determined to live up to the larger than life reputation of his former Prez, Cross. "Same old dream of the day I lost my team. Only difference was that Hazel, the new girl, was dead in my arms, not my team."

Even now, nearly a week later I couldn't figure out why.

"Is she in trouble or the kind of woman who brings trouble with her wherever she goes?" Gunnar laughed at his insight and smacked his thigh in amusement. "You've got the hots for Hazel. She's cute but a little on the quiet side, isn't she?"

Now it was my turn to laugh. "Are we talking about the same woman? The one who has a smartass comment for everything?" *The one who sucked me off like a rockstar?*

"She always shrieks like a damn mouse when I talk to her. I haven't said anything because I thought maybe she'd left some kind of domestic violence situation, and I didn't want it to be fucking weird. Also, because the members love her."

That much was true. When Hazel was behind the bar she wore a big, welcoming smile and charmed everyone who ordered from her.

"They do love her and her personality," I conceded, thinking of how many offers the newest bartender got to join in on the erotic fun. "And I don't have a *thing* for her."

Gunnar was silent for a while but about five miles from Hardtail Ranch he barked out a laugh that startled the fuck out of me.

"Oh, you have a total fucking thing for her and that's fine. Do what you gotta do, Saint. Just don't cost us a bartender, a damn good bartender."

"I won't." I planned to stay as far away from Hazel as humanly possible.

"Good. Because good help is harder to come by than good pussy."

***

"I think it's time I consider getting back out there." The admission shocked even me but as I sat in what passed for Mitch's office these days, a spare room beside Gunnar's home office, I knew the words were true. Some of it had to do with Hazel, but not all of it.

Mitch's brows rose together in confusion. "Out there as in dating? The military? What?"

"The military? I was medically discharged, Mitch."

"I know," he said simply. The sneaky bastard.

I sighed heavily and glanced out the window at the garden that had begun to grow on the side of the house.

Peaches claimed she didn't have a green thumb, but the tomatoes looked red and juicy, the herbs were vibrant and dancing on the breeze and all the other vegetables peeked above ground, temptingly.

"Sex. Relationships. Whatever. That's what I'm thinking about doing, Mitch. Fucking someone other than my hand."

Hell I'd barely even done that this past year.

Mitch nodded, his blue eyes searching me, studying me for any signs of what, I didn't know. "What's brought on this change?"

A groan escaped at that damn question. This is why I hated therapy, all the talking and sharing. It was total bullshit in my opinion and so far hadn't done fuck all to stop the nightmares.

"What brought it on? Other than horny sex dreams about a woman? A particular woman? Can't say, Doc."

Mitch's lips twitched in amusement while he scribbled some notes down on paper. "So Hazel has moved from your nightmares to your fantasies?"

That was one way of putting it. "You could say that."

"Why do you think that is?"

Ugh. "Come on, Doc. Seriously?"

Mitch gave me a long look.

"I don't know, maybe because she's fucking hot. Or maybe it's because I saw her two fingers deep inside her wet cunt, and I haven't stopped thinking about doing it myself. I don't know. You're the doc, you tell me."

"Sounds like you do." He made a few more notes and continued, "Attraction is a good sign, Joplin. It means you're growing. Healing."

"Forgetting is more like it." I hated the thought that one of these days I wouldn't be able to recall the sound of Jank's laugh or that weird dimple that winked when Higgs smiled, or Pony Boy's random encyclopedic knowledge of firearms from around the world. "I can't forget."

"It's not about forgetting, Saint. It's about remembering the good things; the reasons you guys became friends. Brothers."

I nodded knowing he was right but still unable to see through the thick cloud of grief.

"Now about getting out there. Have you thought about how it might feel being so vulnerable at the club with all those people opening up to their deepest desires?"

My shoulders fell because no, I hadn't thought about that and maybe I should have. Every night it was open, The Barn Door was packed with naked, sweaty and gyrating bodies. It was an overload of lights, sounds, and sex. It could easily trigger an episode, which I hadn't had since arriving on Hardtail last year.

"No." But something had to change, didn't it? "I won't know how I'll react if I don't try. Right?" It sounded pathetic, even to my own ears.

WICKED

"That's a good attitude to have, Joplin."

I rolled my eyes at the words he left dangling at the end of that sentence. "But?"

"But this is your place of business as well. Do you really want to risk it?" I didn't know. The truth was my body wanted Hazel but my mind was willing to accept a reasonable facsimile or an equally warm body.

"Maybe start smaller?" his words cut into my thoughts. "One man and one woman."

That was the last damn thing I wanted. One on one was too fucking intimate. It was how things could go wrong, and I couldn't risk that. In a group, everyone would be safe. Probably.

I wanted Hazel. Even thinking about her with her mouth fixed into a little 'O' of pleasure while her fingers, slick with her juices, brought her to climax had me hard. Aching. Dying to get inside of her.

But I couldn't have her one on one. It wasn't safe. Not for me and definitely not for her. "One man and one woman, huh? Sounds like matchmaking to me."

Mitch's lips quirked up, but the smile never fully formed. "Sounds like progress to me. If you're fine with one woman, you'll be fine with three or four."

Maybe Mitch had a point. And maybe he didn't.

Only time and experience would tell.

Chapter Fourteen

Hazel

This was quickly becoming an addiction, showing up early to watch groups of strangers fuck. The men were hard and their bodies sweaty as they thrust their cocks deep into wet pussies, swollen pussies, and tight, slick assholes. Hungry, greedy little mouths. The women were slender and buxom, shy and bold. Some were passive and waited for a big strong cock to tell them what to do—ride it, suck it, take it or feed it to another—while others took a cock, any cock, and had their wicked way with it.

I envied the bold women who could just take what they wanted, whatever fantasy swirled in their head, and worked to make it reality. I even envied the shy women, able to submit and hand their sexual satisfaction over to a complete stranger. They were strong and brave. Unafraid.

And I was on the sidelines. Watching. *Again.*

This was where I wanted to be. Right now, it was where I needed to be. I wasn't ready to go all-in just yet; at least that was what I kept telling myself as my pulse began to race. I watched one of the women get down on her knees in front of two men, taking a cock in each hand before she licked them. One and then the other, her gaze bouncing between the men. My heart thumped in triple time and my breath hitched when the dark haired man wrapped her long ponytail around his fist and slid his cock deep down her throat. Slow and steady until one tiny bead of water slid from her eye.

"Fuck!" The roar of his voice hit me right between the thighs and my clit swelled and my juices flooded my thighs. She slid her tongue against the underside of his cock, and he couldn't hold back the groans of ecstasy. "Shit, yeah baby."

Even his dirty talk did it for me. Lots of swearing and no degradation.

"This is making you hot."

The masculine voice behind me startled me even as it aroused me, his warm breath on my overheated skin.

"Admit it."

Holy fuck! Saint. His voice was low, thick with something that sounded a lot like desire.

"Maybe." I was about to turn when his arm wrapped around my waist and flattened low on my belly.

"Don't turn around. Watch." He spoke barely above a whisper and his words were damn near inaudible with all the moaning and groaning on the platform.

"What's doing it for you, Hazel? The girl sucking that guy off while she gets fucked from behind? Or is the two guys licking one pussy? Yeah, that's the one you like," he said, his fingers rubbing against me when my breath caught in my throat.

His touch lit up my skin like fire, and even though I tried to pretend it didn't affect me, it did. The slide of his thumb, the heat of his breath on the back of my neck, the barest of touch of his lip on my earlobe sent flames of desire coursing through me. Across my chest, down my legs.

I could barely speak, but I made an effort. "I like it as a whole, a-actually."

"Hmm." That growl, so low and gravelly, had me thinking thoughts I shouldn't. Not about Saint. He was my boss, and this was madness. But when he stepped in closer, I wanted the madness.

"So...are you wet right now, Hazel?"

"Am I?" I couldn't stop the small smile that curled my lips involuntarily at playing the game again. This was the fun part. The part where all anybody wanted was a good time. I held my breath and waited to see if Saint would take the bait. Arching my back just in case he didn't get the hint.

He slipped one thick finger under my panties and between my lips. I let out a loud exhale as I felt it inside me, the wetness coating his hand.

"So. Fucking. Wet." He pulled his finger out and slid two in deeper. I gasped and my legs trembled when he pulled away. Again. He murmured in my ear. "Sweet too."

Holy fuck. I knew there was something dark and twisted about him, but I figured it was just stuff leftover from the war. This was...*sinful*.

"Not too sweet I hope?"

"I'd need a proper taste to know that."

I shivered at the thought and suddenly, I wished I were ready.

"For now, tell me what you're looking at, Hazel."

I took in the action in front of me, and my gaze kept going back to the petite redhead now getting two cocks—one in her pussy and one in her ass–while she took eight inches down her throat. I could hear her moan every step of the way. Her pink nipples grew hard, eyes rolling back in ecstasy.

"Her," I groaned. "The redhead." I gasped again when his finger invaded my pussy, plunging so deep my back arched because my greedy pussy wanted more.

"Three cocks, is that your fantasy?" My eyes closed as his fingers worked me, a slow drugging rhythm that was slowly driving me out of my mind. Like the tiny redhead, my nipples were hard against the black silk dress I'd worn with nothing but four-inch heels that were five years old.

"No, you don't want three cocks. You just want one that does it all, right?"

I nodded and bit back a moan when he started to move faster, in and out, in and out. My pussy fluttered as pleasure worked its way up my body, pulsed through my blood. Saint held me close with one hand, the vibration of his words only enhancing the building orgasm.

"Such a tight little pussy for a freak. I wish this was my cock you were squeezing. You're so wet, so hot. Come all over my hand. Come, Hazel."

WICKED

"Please." The word slipped from my lips as pleasure washed over me and vibrated my body until I almost fell over. My body shook and Saint held me, his fingers still tapping my G-spot, wringing every last drop of pleasure he could from my body.

"Fuck, I love to hear you beg. That smart little mouth, begging me to make you come."

"You did a good job," I told him when I finally could speak again, could form words like a normal human. "A damn good job. Even I can't make myself come that quick."

A deep chuckle sounded right beside my ear and his teeth sank into that delicate strip of flesh.

"Good to know. Maybe you learned a few things about yourself." His fingers finally slipped from my trembling body and I whimpered.

I fucking *whimpered!*

I did, dammit. Watching an orgy while someone else made me come was even hotter than my own hand. "Maybe I did." Like maybe I'd add this little encounter to my spank bank for when I needed a quick orgasm in the middle of the day.

"Did you lick your fingers yet?"

"No. Why?"

I sucked in a breath and closed my eyes. "I want to watch you." I needed to watch. This man had been in far too many of my fantasies lately for me to pass up a prime opportunity like this.

"Turn around."

I did and his green eyes hit me like a punch in the gut, dark and filled with the kind of lust I had no business being so close to. He lifted two fingers to his mouth, running them along his bottom lip which he then licked, making my pussy pulse and throb, turned on all over again. Then he stuck both fingers in his mouth, sucking loud enough for me to hear, pulling out clean, slick fingers with a *pop*.

"Fuck me."

His lips curled up into a smile, and I noticed his bottom lip was just that much plumper than the top. Perfect for biting.

"Soon," he whispered. Then Saint took a step back and then another until he disappeared somewhere between the blind spot and the door.

Holy fucking shit! Did that just happen? Did I just let my grumpy, kind of hates me, sexy as a motherfucker boss, finger fuck me to orgasm while I watched a chick getting gangbanged?

Fuck yeah, I did. Nothing could top the night, I was sure of that, but I stayed and watched anyway, riveted by the redhead having the orgasm of her life, convulsing and screaming, squirting all over the place while we all watched in awe. With an imaginary nod of my head, I took one last, longing look and stepped away.

It was time to get to work.

Chapter Fifteen

Saint

The teasing was killing me. It was slowly tearing me apart from the inside out, the sexy low-lidded looks Hazel sent over her shoulder just to make sure I had a good long look at her heart-shaped ass. The way she wiggled her ass against me as we passed each other in the small space behind the bar, making sure her hands always rode low on my stomach or brushed across my chest slow enough to tempt me.

It was a goddamn recipe for disaster, and fucked up fool that I was, I couldn't stay away. Couldn't resist the chance to tease Hazel right back with soft touches and accidental brushes of my own. They affected her. I knew they did because she might have been able to hide her emotions, but she couldn't hide those hard-tipped nipples or that soft intake of breath whenever our skin touched.

We were both playing with fire and equally powerless to stop tempting fate to incinerate us. After making her come while she watched that tiny redhead take three cocks at once. Fuck had that only been a couple of days ago? I was dying for another taste of Hazel. A proper taste this time.

The worst part was that she still invaded my dreams. Time that was meant just for me, to punish me for not being able to save my friends, to remember them, to relive those dark traumatic moments when I wasn't sure if I would live or die.

She was always there. Sometimes it was just her face, lifeless and pale as the life drained out of her. Other times, she was laid out, naked and tempting me beyond all reason to do dirty, wicked things to her, and she promising to do even more to me.

I wanted Hazel to do those things, and I wanted to do them to her too, but I worried Mitch was more right than he knew. What if I tried, and she ended up hurt by me? I couldn't handle that shit, not right now.

Which meant I had to keep my distance. No matter how hard it was.

No matter how hard she made me.

Tonight she wore a black leather skirt with a white lace top and black stilettos that had me thinking about those shoes up in the air while I made the sexy little bartender scream my name.

"Boss," she said in that husky with desire voice that seemed to be her default, hand lightly gripping my bicep. "We're low on straws so I'm going to get some. Be back in five."

She sashayed away, completely covered but looking hot as fuck and sinful as ever. I wanted to follow her with every fiber in my being to extinguish this unquenchable desire she stirred in me.

"Don't do it," Cruz said from my side. Another testament to how much Hazel had me on the hook because I didn't even notice him there. "Women are trouble. Especially the dark ones. Like her."

His head nodded in the direction where Hazel had disappeared. Cruz made a damn good point, but the fact was that no one, not even a woman, a commanding officer, or therapist had gotten me interested in living again the way Hazel had. Hell, not even the Reckless Bastards had revived me the way she had. But I had glimpsed that same darkness Cruz spoke off, and it did have me worried. Still.

"Maybe so, but I find that I like her brand of trouble."

His lips twitched and those big blue eyes sparkled with mischief and amusement.

"I figured that's what you might say. I'll cover the bar, but Gunnar wants to meet in fifteen minutes."

I smiled, tossed the towel I used to wipe down the bar into the back counter and walked away. Right towards trouble.

I found Hazel exactly where I knew she'd be, bending over while she searched the bottom shelf for the straws. Her ass wiggled temptingly, making my mouth water but not as much as the smooth expanse of bare legs on display. I wondered if she had on panties tonight, or if I slid up behind her and pushed her skirt up, would her pretty pink cunt smile back at me, glistening and pulsing. Unable to help myself, I did step closer and wrapped my hands around her thighs, sliding up slowly and enjoying that shocked gasp when she looked at me over her shoulder.

"We have to stop meeting like this," she said, her voice breathy and shaky. Her body already trembling with need.

I let my hands slide up her thighs a little more until my thumbs found plump lips, bare plump lips, swollen and ready. For me.

"I don't know, I kind of like meeting like this." I liked having her at a disadvantage like this. Hell, just the thought of how close I was to her had me hard and aching.

Hazel wiggled again and then straightened, turning so her pebbled nipples brushed against my chest. "Oh yeah?"

Her words were teasing, playful, but I wasn't feeling either of those things. What I felt was dark and foreboding, hungry. Raw. Needy.

"Yeah," I told her; my voice thick with a carnal growl. "Fuck yeah," I clarified and crashed my mouth down on hers, devouring her with every sweep of my tongue until she trembled. Clung to me and rubbed those sweet curves against every inch of me.

She moaned into my mouth, and I was lost to her taste, to the feel of her and the way she gave herself over to pleasure so easily.

"That mouth," she moaned when my lips skidded to her jawbone and down her neck until my tongue dipped inside the hollow at the base of her throat where she tasted like sweat and perfume and something darkly sensual and uniquely Hazel.

"Tell me to stop and I will." It was the only way this would end, if she pushed me away and told me to fuck off. I couldn't walk away, not with my cock straining for her like a goddamn homing beacon. Not with my reaction to Hazel brushing her knuckles over my hard on.

Bottomless eyes held mine as uncertainty and fear swam in them. I wondered what caused the fear, but I was too far gone to give a fuck and Hazel was made of stronger stuff than that, shaking off the fear as she rested a leg over my hip.

"Come closer, Saint. Closer," she whispered when we were toe to toe. "Not close enough," she moaned and licked her lips.

"Hazel." I didn't know what else to say so I said nothing, watching her hands make quick work of my belt, zipper and button so she could plunge in and wrap her dainty hands around my cock.

"So fucking big." She looked up at me and licked her lips. "I remember just how you taste, Saint." Her soft hands stroked me, gentle at first but with more and more force until my control snapped.

"You dream of eating my cock?" It was crude but Hazel didn't mind, her eyes grew wide even as she continued to stroke me. "What else?"

She growled and squeezed me tighter, bringing me right to the edge where I could feel the heat of her pussy calling to me.

"Fuck me, Saint. Hard and fast. Now." I lifted her leg so the tip of my cock slid into her panty-less pussy, and I bit back a curse, pumping my hips in a slow, hypnotic thrust until she took all of me.

"Oh fuck, yes!"

I smiled and lifted her other leg over my hip so she was off the ground completely, nothing but gravity and my cock keeping us fused together. Hazel hooked her legs together behind me, pussy pulsing and leaking all around me as I lost myself in her body.

"Oh fuck, such a tight little cunt."

She laughed and squeezed me tighter, wrapping her arms around my neck and pumping her hips into me.

"Such a big, thick cock. Fuck me, Saint. Fuck me hard."

Dark eyes held mine until I could see the truth of her statement, the dark desire to have me fuck her brutally.

"Please."

It was that plea that broke my resolve, and I swung her around until I found that fucking useless bench Gunnar insisted belonged in this tiny ass space, secretly grateful for his stubbornness because it gave me the perfect place to lay her out.

"You make me crazy."

She smiled but it didn't reach her eyes. "Please, Saint."

As she closed her eyes, I gripped her thighs and held them apart so I could see the way her pussy glistened, the way her clit pulsed with desire as I pulled out and pumped into her again and again, harder and faster, harder and deeper, harder and harder still while her hands clawed at my chest, my back. My ass.

"Oh fuck!" Her heels dug into my ass, urging me to fuck her even harder. I wasn't sure if I could, even though I wanted to get lost in her body until I forget everything but the feel of her cunt clamped around my cock.

"Fuck. Hazel!"

I gripped her tits in my hand, squeezing hard as I fucked her so hard the bench moved a few inches at a time. No matter how hard I fucked Hazel, she begged for more. Eyes clenched tight, she begged for more cock, harder cock. A harder fuck.

"Fuck me, Saint!"

My hands slid up from her tits, enjoying the feel of her silky smooth skin, slick with arousal and effort. She wrapped her hands around my wrist and moved them until they were at her throat.

"Hazel?"

"Please," she growled and her pussy squeezed me so tight that a blast of vibrant lights went off behind my eyes.

It didn't feel right to do what she wanted but my cock plunged in and out of her body, giving her everything she wanted. I knew I was powerless to deny her even this. I wrapped my hand around her throat and applied pressure gently, still fucking her but not as hard as before.

"Saint," she growled. "Do it. Don't fucking stop."

Ah, fuck. Her pussy flooded with moisture, proof to the fact that this was her weird fucking kink and nothing more. She was getting off on having my fingers around her throat while my cock punished her, so who was I to deny her? I squeezed again and her lips curled into a smile, her cunt pulsed and vibrated around me.

Following her lead, I applied as much pressure as she could stand, all the while fucking her like a mindless drone, hard and rough and fast, even as she begged for more.

"Yes," she choked out and opened her eyes. "More."

Her feet urged me forward and her nails dug into my skin until I bled, but I never stopped. At some point my body took over, thrusting hard and deep while my hand held her throat, at the mercy of my own fucking desire.

That thought ripped away another layer, and I gave Hazel exactly what she wanted and how she wanted it. Soon her body trembled and shook, convulsed as she arched towards me and a violent orgasm exploded from her, milking my cock like she couldn't get enough of it.

"Fuck yes! Fuck yes!" A wicked smile curled her lips as she continued to shake, yanking my orgasm from me, interrupting the wild bucking of my hips into her body.

Holy. Shit. My body shook violently as the orgasm erupted out of me, my hips still moving into her as pleasure flooded her body, making her choke. When I could think straight again, I let go of her neck, opened my eyes and stared at her as she stared back at me, clearly feeling the same shock I had.

"Damn. You're a hot fuck."

"Yeah," she agreed and sat up as I separated our bodies, her breath still coming in choppy and short. "Worth it."

I frowned. "Worth what?" Was this when she would attempt blackmail or some other favor from me?

"The weirdness sure to follow," she said and stood, reaching for a package of bar napkins, presumably to clean away the evidence of me dripping down her leg.

I glanced at my watch and groaned. "I gotta go. Meeting with Gunnar," I explained even though I didn't owe her an explanation.

"Sure," she snorted and shook her head before she turned away from me. "And I've got drinks to sling. See you around, Saint."

Not knowing what else to say, I put my cock back in my pants and left the storage room on shaky legs and a still-leaking cock.

A shit-eating grin curved my lips as I made my way to the Sin Room that Gunnar sometimes called Church. I'd managed to fuck a woman to orgasm with no reminders of the past. No flashbacks. No danger.

Just pleasure.

What a fucking concept.

***

"There was another robbery last night," Gunnar said as his gaze landed on each and every one of us, making sure we all understood the seriousness of the matter now.

"This time those fuckers sent Edna Mae to the hospital with a broken hip."

He bit out another curse and smashed his fist down on the table.

I understood his anger. Edna Mae was good people. Hell, she was a quintessential small town woman. Widowed for years with more money than she knew what to do with, the woman opened up a yarn and sewing shop where women of all ages gathered to gossip and complain in private. I went in there by accident one day and since then, she'd made me two sweaters, a scarf and a hat because according to Edna, ranch life got cold in winter, even in Texas.

"Shit. Is Edna all right?"

All eyes turned to me, some questioning but only Cruz smiled, because he knew the truth. Gunnar nodded. "A broken hip ain't no walk in the park for a chick her age, but word is she's already giving the doctors and nurses hell."

That made me smile. A world where Edna Mae wasn't a seventy year old spitfire was a world I wanted no part of. Ever. "What happened?"

"Those assholes didn't realize that unlike the other condos in the area, Edna's is connected to the inside of her shop. She heard the commotion and came down with her shotgun. The recoil sent the old girl tumbling down the last few steps. Hard."

It was clear that Gunnar held the robbers responsible more than her age or perceived clumsiness, and I agreed with him. Those fuckers were going down.

"What do you want to do?" It was time to discuss this as a club, what our options actually were as well as the repercussions.

"First thing is recon," Gunnar said simply, his military training kicking in admirably, or maybe it was his years spent as a solider in a different type of army. "We need to get on a regular rotation so maybe we can catch these fuckers in the act. That's our first priority."

Wheeler nodded and leaned back in his chair. "What do we know for certain?"

Gunnar recapped the robberies in town, the way Big Mac had been roughed up and now Edna Mae, hospitalized.

"Saint and I went through town the other night and he thinks it's a group of at least two, maybe four or more."

All eyes swung to me, and I cursed to myself, silently wishing Gunnar had just left my name out of it. Calling me a fucking Sergeant at Arms didn't make it so, didn't make me any kind of fucking enforcer, not when I was too fucked up in the head to do the job. Gunnar's blue gaze seared through mine, encouraging me to speak up. These guys were supposedly my brothers, my family. But this was all new to me.

If I wanted this life then I would have to do more than hope for the fucking best so I took a deep breath and nodded.

"The front windows are broken but it's not how they got in so we have to assume it's a diversion, especially because all the business that've been hit, have back entrances with no surveillance and almost no visibility."

The Sin Room fell silent for so long my gaze fell to the table and butterflies took up residence in my gut. I knew I shouldn't have said anything, should have just kept my mouth shut and let them figure it out without me.

Slayer broke the silence. "Hot damn! He speaks!" He accompanied his smartass comment with a wide, satisfied smile.

Holden's lips twitched. "We were beginnin' to wonder aboutcha, boy."

I smirked. "I got your boy."

I wondered if they thought I was solid enough, stable enough, to be part of their family. Or was it something else?

"It's just a guess."

"Wrong," Wheeler said, his gaze serious and sober. "It's a damn good theory of what happened, and we'll all keep an eye out for that on shift."

Gunnar nodded. "Wheeler and Slayer will take tonight's shift, and we'll figure it out for the rest of the week. I want these fuckers found before someone else gets hurt."

The unspoken part of that statement was that he—or *we*—would fuck them up bad when we found them.

Because we would. Of that I had no fucking doubt. "And the cops?"

Gunnar grinned and swung his gaze to Wheeler. "Wheeler's gonna stop by OPD and make a huge donation on behalf of Hardtail Ranch."

Wheeler blinked slowly and flashed a knowing grin. "And how big will this donation be, Prez?" His blue eyes filled with amusement as he stared at Gunnar.

"Big enough that they'll come running if there's any trouble out this way."

Despite his relative newness as a leader, Gunnar had the skills to get the job done. We'd all had our fair share of useless fucking leaders out on the battlefield, those who had done more to contribute to failure and death than to success, but Gunnar, he was the kind of leader people dreamed about. The kind who would be first to take fire, which made it a hell of a lot easier to take orders from him.

And he was so fucking cool.

"On it," he said and stood, turning a gaze to Slayer. "We'll leave in an hour. The businesses will all be about to shut down by then, so maybe we'll get some intel through the Opey grapevine."

Slayer laughed. "We'll get more than that. The women in this town have excellent taste. Young or old, they all love me."

We all groaned because Slayer had no problem telling us all how he'd gained his nickname. He was the Pussy Slayer after all—and dammit if he wasn't right. There were people who could talk to animals, to assholes, to kids. But Slayer had a way with the opposite sex, and I had no doubt he'd get us the info we needed.

"Well, maybe get the details before you stick your dick in one of 'em," Holden grumbled and stood beside the door, clearly ready for the meeting to end.

Slayer flashed a smile and clapped Holden on the back. "Don't be upset Mah-Dick, you've still got the biggest cock around. By a few inches, too."

Holden glared at him and pushed him away. "Asshole."

"All right, kids," Cruz shouted with a wide grin. "You all have very pretty cocks. Just not as fine as mine."

That started another round of jokes and insults that made me feel, just for a second, that I was right back with my unit, joking around and shooting the shit. Giving each other a hard time because we were men and that was how we related to one another.

The meeting broke up, and I made my way back upstairs, toward the thumping bass and grinding bodies, toward the far too tempting bartender, all while my thoughts stayed on the robbery crew. They weren't after drugs, at least not yet since they hadn't hit the pharmacy, but they weren't just being a fucking menace. This crew had a goal and until we figured it out, we'd keep on being a step behind.

That was un-fucking-acceptable.

Chapter Sixteen

Hazel

"What in the ever lovin' fuck?" The drive home from The Barn Door took longer than usual thanks to a few stray cows deciding that the dead of night was the perfect time to go for a stroll in the middle of the road. If not for the mind-melting orgasm I'd had in the storage room and three hundred and seventy-five bucks in tips I made tonight, the next crazy sight in front of me would have pissed me right the fuck off.

Police tape stretched from one end of the large picture window that belonged to Edna Mae's business, Spin A Yarn, all the way to the door that I used to enter my apartment. Which meant my day wasn't over.

Yet.

Fuck. Me.

The broken glass and police tape were out of the ordinary in Opey, but the flashing lights had me looking up once again to make sure I hadn't taken a wrong turn and ended up in some alternate universe. Curiosity over what had happened and the old woman's status warred with exhaustion, and I tiptoed around the back entrance, hoping for a miracle. Where the front entrance was well-lit and difficult to discern if it was a business or private entrance, the back was dark and scary and clearly not a commercial location.

I climbed the stairs slowly, ignoring the crunch of what was probably a broken lightbulb as I made my way up, on the lookout for any signs of danger.

"Motherfucker!" Beside Edna's door, which she only used to stop by and offer me leftovers and unwanted gossip, my own door had been kicked open, leaving splintered wood littering the hall floor.

"Ma'am?" A young officer with short blond hair and rosy red cheeks stepped out of Edna's place. "You can't go in there. This whole place is a crime scene."

A crime scene? In Opey? "What do you mean a crime scene, I live here. Where is Edna Mae? Is she all right?"

WICKED

The old woman had been nothing but nice and welcoming since I arrived in town, telling me all about her Earle and their life together, her retirement from teaching and even the origins of the town. She didn't ask a lot of questions either, which made her the perfect neighbor as far as I was concerned.

"I'm sorry for the inconvenience, but someone broke into Edna's shop and they left a huge mess." He was saying something else but I didn't give a shit. Edna was a kind woman and she'd been more helpful than my own landlord, some asshole who didn't even live in town.

"Where is Edna?"

He sighed again. "She broke her hip."

"No!" Another of life's lessons that I'd hoped to outrun. Bad shit always happened to good people who didn't deserve it while the shitty people went on, enjoying their lives.

"Shit, poor Edna Mae."

The officer flashed a sympathetic smile. "We're all broken up about it, but I'm afraid you can't get in there until after the crime scene guys are finished and they won't be here for an hour. At least."

An hour. An hour for a person with tons of friends, or even one friend, was no problem to fill. For me, it meant at least sixty minutes of boredom. And hunger because everything was closed and the only food I had was in my fridge.

"What about clothes, can I get a change?"

That sympathetic smile was the only answer he gave. No, I couldn't get inside the place I've been working my ass off to pay for, not until the crime scene guys had come through.

Just. Fucking. Great.

"Thanks, Officer." There was no reason to give him attitude, even though I really wanted to put this frustration on someone. Anyone. Instead I turned around and went back down the pitch black, glass covered stairwell, and made my way out into the chilly, night air. Since I was barely dressed, I slid back into my car and sat behind the wheel for at least fifteen minutes. My mind wandered. To Edna Mae. To work. To Jessie. To the orgasm I had earlier, and especially to the man who'd given me that pleasure.

With my head bowed on the steering wheel, I took several deep breaths and tried to clear my mind. I could take my tips and grab a few items from the convenience store on the outskirts of town and check into a motel. At least a motel would come with a hot shower and some privacy to satisfy the desire thinking about Saint caused to rise up in me.

Damn, who knew a man who ran so hot and cold could be so fucking hot?

A knock on my driver's side window startled me, and I reached for the piece I kept under the driver's seat for long drives late at night. I looked up into familiar laughing brown eyes. Long chocolate hair and a matching beard should have made him intimidating, but with his smile and charm, Slayer was just a big presence. I rolled the window a couple inches and arched a brow. "Yes?"

"What's going on?"

I shrugged and gave him a rundown on the Edna Mae situation.

"She's my neighbor and they kicked my door in too before they realized I don't have shit worth stealing. So I'm waiting for the crime scene techs to come and go. What are you doing here?"

"Just driving by," he said with a casual ease I didn't believe for a second. "You know it'll be more than an hour, right?"

"Probably, but it is what it is." Spending my money on a motel was less appealing by the minute. "Don't worry about me, Slayer, this isn't the first time I've slept in my car."

The look on his face turned fierce. "Maybe not, but you don't need to tonight. We have a bunkhouse at Hardtail with some empty beds."

It was a nice gesture but keeping a clear barrier between work and personal was something I was working on. "That's not necessary. Thanks for the offer, but I won't be putting anyone out."

"Stubborn," he mumbled under his breath, flashing a smile at me when I glared at him. "Look, you're not putting anybody out. We have room at the ranch. So no one is moving out for you."

That was better, but did I really want to stay with my coworkers? Or worse, my boss' friends? No, but I also didn't want to sleep in my car with armed robbers on the loose. "You sure Gunnar won't mind?"

Slayer looked over his shoulder, where I noticed the pretty one, Wheeler, talking on the phone. He was as big and rugged as the rest of the guys, but he was so goddamn beautiful it was disturbing. Wheeler gave a short nod and turned away from us.

"I'm sure," Slayer said. "He insists, actually."

"That would be great," I said on a sigh. "Thank you."

"No problem. We take care of our own." He winked and took a step back.

I frowned at his words. "I work for you guys, but I still appreciate the offer."

"Since no one else is offering you a place to stay, I'd say you're one of us. Smartass."

I glared at him and he laughed, shrugging in his patented carefree way. "Do you need anything from upstairs?"

"Plenty, but I can't get in right now so I'm ready." As ready as I would ever be.

***

The bunkhouse was, thankfully, empty. And quiet. Though the place was huge, Slayer had put me on the east side of the building which was completely unoccupied save for a few bunk beds. All empty with the mattresses rolled up and no bedding to be found.

WICKED

Anywhere.

It was a nice gesture despite the bareness of it all, and I dropped down on the lone single bed with a loud sigh that seemed to echo in the room. It was four o'clock in the morning, and I still hadn't been to sleep yet, and worse, it wouldn't come easy. Or at all tonight.

Not having a place to stay, to lay my head at night, was really getting to me even though this was nothing like all the other times I'd been homeless in my life. It felt the same, being at the mercy of a stranger's goodwill, which I knew all too well came with plenty of strings. It made me antsy. Anxious. I stood and paced the length of the room, still in my black 'fuck me' stilettos, trying to get my mind and heart to stop racing. Stop spinning.

To settle the fuck down so I could think straight. A shower, that was what I needed first, but I had no soap, no towels and no clothes to change in to, so I threw myself back on the bed and closed my eyes. Sleep still didn't come, but I didn't expect it would.

"Knock, knock!" A feminine voice sounded, drawing my attention to the hall that connected the east and west wings of the bunkhouse. "Hazel, are you in here?"

I sat up and then stood, suddenly alarmed. "Yeah. Who's asking?"

A beautiful bi-racial woman with wild copper curls came in with two big ass bags and a wide grin on her face. "I'm Peaches, Gunnar's almost wife. I heard you might need some bare necessities, and I came to help."

Peaches. I'd heard a lot about her. She was some expert hacker who'd gotten tangled up with corrupt government agents. The guys had provided her with a safe haven. That was the extent of what I knew about her, and no one had mentioned how beautiful she was.

"Uh, thank you. This is really helpful at four o clock in the fucking morning."

"I'm a helpful girl," she said and lifted the checkered bag on one of the beds, pulling out bedding that looked soft and clean and comfortable.

"Gunnar said you were small so my stuff won't fit you, lucky bitch, but I have some things to get you through the next few days. Or we could get up early tomorrow and go shopping. Whatever works for you."

Her smile was welcoming and I felt my shoulders start to relax.

"Thank you, Peaches. I'd love that, but I can't spend my tip money until I find out whether or not those fuckers took my stash." No foster kid ever kept money in the bank because it was easy to take away, and I was no different. I kept a small mobile safe that required a code and a fingerprint to open, but they could have taken it.

"Your place got hit too?"

"Don't know. Couldn't get in." The thought that all that money I'd saved over the past few weeks had been stolen made me want to throw up. "Fuck."

"No honey, fuck that. We're going to get your money. Now." Peaches stared me down with her arms crossed and a serious as fuck expression on her face.

I wavered at first, but she must have sensed my desperation because Peaches was there when I stepped out of the shower, keys dangling from her fingers.

"I guess we're going," I told her with a shaky but grateful smile.

Twenty minutes later we had crept into my apartment, which had crime scene tape zigzagging across the entrance.

"Don't touch anything but the safe," Peaches whispered around the tiny penlight between her teeth. She was an expert all right, and her skills went far beyond hacking.

"How'd you learn to pick a lock?"

She grinned up at me with a shrug. "Misspent youth in foster care."

"Really? You don't seem…" I didn't know how to finish that statement without offending her so I snapped my mouth shut.

"Like a foster kid? Oh believe me, I've got my coping skills and shit, but I'm as fucked up as the rest. Jealous?"

"Been there, done that."

The door opened, and we were inside like cat burglars, crawling on the floor so we wouldn't draw any attention from the patrol car out front. I found the safe under the loose floorboard under my creaky ass bed, untouched. Still stacked with thousands of dollars in cash.

My safety net. My rainy day fund. "Got it!"

She smiled and tugged me out of the apartment before I could grab a few creature comforts.

"We can go shopping later, as long as we don't get caught in here." She had a point and though my shoulders fell in disappointment, I let her drag me out.

"It's late—or early—enough that we could get breakfast now. Martha has Maisie so I have the time."

"I've got nothing else on my agenda," I told her with a half-smile, and we headed for the all-night place on the edge of town.

Peaches dropped down in a back booth, and we ordered more food than anyone would consider ladylike. Luckily, neither of us claimed to be ladies.

"So Hazel, how'd you end up in Opey?"

I shrugged. "My best friend who's more like my sister fell in love and got married. I left her in Oklahoma. I wanted to do something with my life and somehow ended up in Texas."

I left out the fact that there had been several stops over the years along the way.

"I have one of those. Vivi. I didn't want to leave her either, but with bad guys chasing me and her being knocked up, I had to book it out of town. I miss her like hell, though."

"Me, too," I admitted just before the waitress arrived with our food. "How'd you meet Gunnar? You guys seem so different."

He was gruff and borderline grouchy all the damn time and Peaches seemed to be a bottle of fucking sunshine.

She laughed. "He's a grumpy bastard, isn't he? Hated me on sight the moment I met him. Vivi is married to one of his brothers in the MC."

"MC?"

"Motorcycle club. Back in Mayhem. It's a small town by Las Vegas. He just started the Opey chapter of the Reckless Bastards MC. I thought you knew."

I shook my head, surprised as shit because I expected bikers to be big bad, leather wearing motherfuckers who cussed a lot and treated woman as disposable objects. Because that was what the bikers were like during the five months I'd spent working at a biker bar. "They don't seem like the sort." Especially Saint.

"They aren't. They're *Harley enthusiasts*." She said with air quotes. "And more like family. Just like the club in Mayhem, these guys are all vets. They served their country and lost themselves in the process. Through the biker club, they get a little of it back."

"Sounds kind of nice, actually." It made sense why many foster kids ended up in gangs or cults. The need to belong was more powerful than any drug.

"It is. And if you let them, they'll welcome you right into the fold."

I shook my head. "I can't afford to do that."

If I got too close to people, I'd set myself up for a world of hurt. It was a lesson I'd learned too many times to forget now, at the ripe old age of twenty-six.

"I've got Jessie when we find the time, but at this point, I'm used to being on my own."

"Bullshit," she said with a sweet smile. "It's easier to be alone, that's for sure. I was alone for many years. Until the shit hit the fan, and I had no one to lean on when I desperately needed it." Her eyes took on a faraway quality that said she was thinking of her own need.

"Yeah but that's easier to accept than expecting someone to be there when you need them, only to have them disappoint you."

I was the one person I knew wouldn't let me down so that was who I let myself lean on. Period.

"Good point. I'll just say this and then I'll shut up. At some point you'll have to trust someone."

"I trust people as I need to."

Peaches sighed and pushed some of the curls off her face. "Okay, well you can trust me and maybe we can even become friends."

That sounded nice, but I wasn't good at making or keeping friends. "You seem like you have plenty of friends."

She laughed. "I have Vivi, Maisie and the guys."

It was more than I had. "That doesn't sound so bad. Who's Maisie?"

"Gunnar's sister. She's a little kid and as a big girl, I need some *big girl* friends."

Her honesty was refreshing and I found that I liked Peaches.

"I'm a terrible friend, but I'm game if you are."

She accepted my words and paid the bill before we set off for Hardtail Ranch. Peaches made her way to the main house and I headed toward the bunkhouse.

Where Saint was waiting with a dark look on his handsome face.

Chapter Seventeen

Saint

"You here to see me?"

Hazel didn't give off the stalker vibe but the crazy ones never broadcasted their intentions until it was too late and even though my cock was already stirring in my jeans at the sight of her, I knew I had to play it cool.

She stopped short, hands loaded with bags, leaving her body fully on display. Even in baggy clothes, those sinful curves peeked out and made me lick my lips.

"No, I'm not," she huffed. "My apartment is next to Edna Mae's, and I can't be there, so one of your buddies told me there was an empty bed in the bunkhouse. Is this gonna be a problem?"

Hell yeah, it was. How in the hell would I keep my hands off her when we were in a room filled with beds? Even now my fingers twitched to reach out and grab a handful of hair until she had no choice but to drop down to her knees and open her mouth to me.

"Not for me."

"Good. I won't be here long," she said, her dark eyes boring into me, daring me to tell her the truth, to tell her that she couldn't stay here.

"A few days. Tops."

"Don't hurry on my account." My lips curled into a slow smile that made Hazel roll her eyes.

"Right." She went out of her way to avoid touching me, which made me smile.

"Are you all right?"

"I'm fine," she said automatically in a flat voice that said she was used to handling things on her own. Exclusively on her own.

"I'll take this side," she said, dumping her stuff on one of the beds. She kept her back to me, which I didn't mind since it gave me a clear view of that round, heart shaped ass. It really was a great ass.

"Did they steal anything?" The thought of her place, her personal space being violated pissed me off and my hands balled into fists at my sides.

"Not that I could tell. They didn't take the thing I was most concerned about so it's no big deal."

"What were you most concerned about?"

"The safe where I keep my cash." Again, her words were matter of fact, devoid of emotion.

"How did you get it if your place is a crime scene?" She didn't strike me as a woman who'd take the risk after the cops told her to leave, which told me just how much that money meant to her.

"I have my ways. All that matters is that it's safe and back where it belongs." Finally she turned around, fire burning in her brown eyes as she crossed her arms and stared at me. "I already told you that I don't plan to stick around long, Saint. What's going on?"

"I just want to make sure you're all right. Nothing more. Is that a problem?"

"It's not a problem, I'm just wondering where this concern is coming from all of a sudden? Most days you seem to hate me, so excuse the skepticism."

"Hate you? Is that what you think? My life would be a hell of a lot easier if I hated you, Hazel."

I don't know what possessed me to say that, but it was already out there, and I couldn't take it back. "I don't hate you."

"Good, because I haven't done anything for you to hate me, but for the record, I can take care of myself, Saint."

I grinned and held my hands up. "Never said you couldn't."

"I know that," she said automatically, a hint of sadness in her voice. "I just mean that you don't need to worry about me."

"Maybe I want to worry about you."

Her eyes flashed wide and wary as I bridged the distance between us, not stopping until I could see the little pulse at the base of her neck, pounding a hard rock beat of arousal.

"And I'm telling you that you don't need to. I'm a big girl and I can take care of myself, Saint."

"They aren't mutually exclusive, you know."

She was a tough girl, not just playing at it like some of the lost souls I've come across working The Barn Door, or just hanging out in dark places where people wanted to forget who they were and the things they did.

"I want you to be careful Hazel."

"I always am. What happened had nothing to do with me so you don't need to worry that I'll bring some unsavory element to the club."

My lips curled into a grin. "You've got me all figured out, don't you?"

"No, I don't." She stepped back to put some distance between us but found herself sandwiched between me and one of the bunks. "But I know you run the club so I'm telling you before you can ask, that I'm not the source."

"Again, I didn't think you were. Wow. So defensive," I told her and slid a finger down the curve of her jaw, lightly gripping her chin so she couldn't look away. "I wonder why that is."

She tried to jerk away but I tightened my hold until her gaze met mine, unable to look away.

"Maybe because I don't know you?"

I laughed at her deflection. "You know me well enough to deepthroat my cock. Well enough to let me finger fuck you, eat you out and fuck you until you could barely walk."

"That's just sex," she insisted. "It's not the same. And I don't want anything from you, so just relax."

"You don't know what you want," I told her and ran a finger across her bottom lip. "If you did, you'd already be naked and begging for this dick."

She sucked in a breath that hit me straight in the cock, making things even harder than they were.

"I know exactly what I want, Saint. You just can't believe that it might not be you."

I let out another laugh and shook my head, stepping in even closer so my chest brushed against hers. She was so fucking soft, felt as good as she smelled, and I wanted to be as close as possible. Hell, I wanted to bury myself deep into her wet pussy until her fingernails broke my skin and she forgot her name.

"You want me, I know that. Without a doubt. What I can't figure out," I whispered the words in her ear and tugged her earlobe between my teeth until she hissed out a breath, "is why you'd lie about it."

"Maybe because I like my job, Saint. I need my job, and I don't want to lose it because I wasn't clingy enough or standoffish enough afterward."

I could see that truth.

"I wouldn't do that."

I took a step back and slid a hand through my hair. "I would never do that. Shit, I haven't even done any of this in a long damn time. Too long."

"I'll bet you say that to all the girls," she practically purred with a gentle, sweet smile that was at odds with the firmness of her words.

"You're hardly a girl though, are you?" She was a woman, a grown ass woman that my body wanted. Needed on a level that was uncomfortable and honestly, unwelcoming.

"No, I'm not. I'm a grown woman who knows exactly what she wants. And when a man's trying to fuck her. That's what all this is about, right Saint? You want to fuck me again."

She shook her head and mumbled under her breath as she yanked open her jeans and shoved them down over her hips.

"That's all you had to say, Saint. As you said, I'm a grown woman and I don't need pretty words or false promises."

Before she finished the words, she was naked as the day she was born, chest heaving, nipples hard and her skin was pink and flushed. Beautiful.

I wanted to resist her just to prove a fucking point, that my concern wasn't false or insincere, but those hard pink nipples made my mouth go dry. I couldn't resist the way her belly trembled when I ran a hand from her throat down to the pretty pink slit between her thighs. But I was a weak man, unable to resist the allure she presented, beautiful and angry and aroused.

"Just because I want you, because I can't stop thinking about you, doesn't mean that my concern is insincere." One finger slid through her wet pussy lips and her head fell back as a moan erupted out of her. "You're so fucking wet."

"You seem to have that effect on me," she said, the words came out barely a whisper. Hazel's legs widened just enough that I could slip inside. If I wanted.

"Not yet," I told her as she swirled her hips to get closer, to take more of my finger inside of her.

"I don't play games, Saint." She pushed at my chest and took a step back, or at least she tried to, but I dipped a finger into her pussy and cut off whatever else she'd been about to say.

"Oh fuck!"

My lips curled into a grin at her words, and I took another step closer, wrapping an arm around her waist so I could pull out and plunge two fingers into her.

"You're so fucking wet for me, Hazel. I can feel your pussy clenching and squeezing, greedy. Just. Like. You."

She vibrated in my arms, purring and writhing while I fucked her with my fingers and teased her clit with my thumb.

"Fuck, oh fuck!" She gripped my wrist and rode my hand, and I swear it was the hottest goddamn thing I had ever seen.

"Come for me, Hazel." I was hungry to see her come apart, to feel her pussy squeeze my hands until I lost feeling. I needed to see it again and again, somewhere other than my dreams.

"Make me."

I would have liked to believe it was the challenge in her tone and in her eyes that pushed me, but it wasn't. It was her. The scent of her pussy when she was all hot and bothered and ready to come, got to me in a way even I didn't understand.

"Make me come, Saint."

Okay yeah, maybe it *was* the challenge in her eyes. A little.

"Not yet," I told her and smiled when she growled at me. Hazel was a feisty bitch, and I was learning, a little each day, that I really loved a feisty bitch.

"Dammit, Saint!"

"Oh yeah, now you're ready." I lifted her in the air and threw her down on the nearest bed, enjoying the way her tits jiggled when she landed. My cock grew harder than it had ever been in my whole fucking life, I grinned at her. "Are you ready to come now, Hazel?"

She nodded, a hungry, greedy look in her eyes that I knew I'd never forget in a million years.

I kissed her slowly, from her lips down to the soft skin between her thighs, parting her so I could see the way her pink pussy glistened with arousal. Then my mouth was on her pussy, feasting as her sweet honey coated my tongue. I licked and sucked her clit while my fingers worked her over, in deep quick thrusts that had her panting and crying my name in regular intervals.

"Fuck, your pussy is so sweet."

"Suck. Harder."

My gaze connected with Hazel's, and I gave her exactly what she wanted, sucking her clit so hard she bucked off the bed and smacked against my face, but still I didn't stop. I nibbled her clit and sucked it, fucking her with two fingers until she was so close I knew one soft blow and she'd be done for.

"Not yet," I told her again and slipped my middle finger deep inside her wet cunt.

"Saint. What the fu—?" Her words were cut off by the feeling of my one long middle finger sliding between her ass cheeks and into that dark star most women pretended to hate.

"Oh fuck," she moaned and bucked against me again, this time not knowing which way to buck.

"Now you're ready," I told her and put my mouth back on her clit, sucking as hard as I fucked her ass with my finger until pleasure erupted out of her, bubbling to the surface with every violent jerk of her body, every cry of pleasure that tore through the air.

"Oh fuck. Oh fuck. Shit, oh fuck!" A nervous laugh escaped, and I continued licking her clit until she began to squirm and then the flutters started.

Again.

I sat up and undressed quicker than I did the first time I showered in the desert, fisting my cock in my hand and shoving into her wet cunt.

"So. Goddamn. Hot." There was nothing better than sliding into a sloppy wet pussy, except sliding into a *hot* wet pussy, and Hazel was right there, gripping my cock inside her cunt's vise grip.

"Oh, Saint..." Her back arched and her heels dug into my back, sending me further into the dark abyss and making me lose all sense of time and control. Hazel gave her body over to me, shouting as I pumped into her pussy hard and fast, keeping up a brutal pace she didn't just tolerate, but enjoyed. "Yes! Please! More."

"Ah, fuck!" My hips moved out of control and seconds later she was coming apart all around my cock, clenching and drenching me in her orgasm. It was a glorious thing to watch, and I got so caught up I barely noticed the volcanic eruption that was my own orgasm.

"Fuck. Me."

"We just did. And we can do this anytime," she said with a smile that almost made me believe her.

Almost.

"I thought you didn't play games."

She froze and her smile faded. "I don't. Just consider it a compliment that your dick scrambled my brains enough that I almost did something stupid."

In the next second her hands were on my chest, pushing me away as she strode to the bathroom, stark naked, and closed the door behind her.

I could've waited her out, and I would have, but Gunnar had called emergency church, and I was already running late.

Hazel would have to wait.

***

"These pricks are escalating." Gunnar stood at the head of the table, back erect and shoulders so broad they seemed to stretch from wall to wall or maybe that was just the breadth of his anger. He gripped the back of his chair so tight his knuckles turned white. "They didn't just put Edna Mae in the hospital and trash Hazel's apartment. No, this time, those motherfuckers committed arson, burning Terrie's Urban Boutique to the ground. This shit is unacceptable. Terrie's a single mom and I know that means something to a lot of us in here. Thankfully she wasn't hurt, but her means of supporting her kids has been fuckin' decimated. Get me?"

Heads nodded all around the table, agreement wafted in the air along with something darker, more intense. Bloodthirst and vengeance. This time I understood perfectly. "Gotcha, Gunnar."

He tilted his head in my direction. "You get it now?"

"I get it, man." I did. This wasn't just about making money, even though the MC would make money providing additional protection to the businesses in town. This was about a way of life. Preserving that way of life for the people who chose to live in our town, because that's what Opey was now. Ours.

"Good. Holden has already set up a donation for Terrie, routed through one of our holding companies so it'll just appear as an anonymous donation. The town already set up one for Big Mac and Edna Mae so we just added a lump sum to help out."

Gunnar was all hell fired up about protecting the town and the more he paced and the more he talked, the more my respect for him grew.

"You don't waste a minute, man." Cruz shook his head, eyes shining with disbelief and admiration.

"None to waste. I had a long talk with the mayor last night at the club. He's a big fucking fan by the way." Gunnar flashed a shit-eating grin as he dropped down into his chair at the head of the table.

"Him and the wifey love our little club, and he wanted us to know that he appreciated the campaign contribution and our efforts to look out for Opey."

Gunnar's plans were coming to life just the way he'd envisioned them. That combined with having a woman to love and the sweetest little girl in the world, no wonder he was walking around with his dick swinging like King Kong.

It all sounded good, but it wasn't the most important part of the equation. "Anybody seen anything on the nightly patrols?"

"No, goddammit." Gunnar flung a pen across the table, anger rolling off of him in waves. "These pricks are slippery as hell. We know they've been around, but we've seen fuck all from them." He pounded a fist into his hand. "I can't wait to get my hands on these motherfuckers."

"Me, too," Slayer said, pounding the table with his fist, angry and ready for vengeance. "Fucking with those businesses and good folks who don't deserve this shit. That's unacceptable."

"Maybe we need to double the patrols," Holden suggested, his deep voice booming throughout the small room. "Cover both sides of town so they can't slip away as easy as they have been."

"As much as we can," I agreed with a shrug of my shoulders. "We need more of a presence in town so we can see who they might be. Take your women out for dinner or dancing, have a drink with some of the guys at the bar. Shit like that."

Gunnar and Holden nodded, the wheels spinning in their heads as plans began to form. It wasn't unlike watching Jank come up with an alternative plan on the fly because nothing ever went how you thought it would in the desert. Apparently, war never fucking ended.

Ever.

"We'll get a plan in place right away. Any volunteers for tonight?"

Gunnar looked around the room, and I knew just what he saw: a bunch of sad sack veterans with no love lives to speak of. Slayer sometimes had overnight visitors of the female variety, but the rest of us were as lonely as the day we set foot on Hardtail Ranch.

"Come on guys, none of you has a woman who'll tolerate your ugly mug in exchange for a free dinner?"

Slayer laughed. "Usually it's the women who buys me dinner, but I guess I can see who wants to ride the pole tonight."

Arms spread wide; he rolled his hips in a lewd gesture that was so typical Slayer that even I laughed.

"I'll go."

The room fell silent as soon as the words left my mouth, all eyes looking at me like I'd grown a third fucking head.

"What? I'm not the biggest motherfucker around, which means people won't notice."

Of all the guys at Hardtail, I was the smallest. Cruz was shorter than me but that fucker was built like a refrigerator, stocky as hell with too many muscles.

"Yeah? And who you gonna take, Saint?"

I knew Wheeler was joking, but it was still goddamn offensive. "Tell us about the woman keeping you distracted these days."

Distracted was a good damn word for it because thoughts of Hazel had distracted me for weeks. Sometimes, at night when I was about to have the nightmare about losing my friends, I welcomed the distraction she brought. Other times, like now, when the scent of her lingered on my skin and my clothes, I cursed her existence.

"I don't know what the fuck you're talking about. I said I'd go."

"Bullshit." Of course Slayer was the one to call me out, because he was far more perceptive than anybody realized. "Not only have you been distracted in the way that could only be from a woman, but right now you smell like you've been buried in pussy for the last few hours."

His lips curved up and spread into a shit-eating grin because the fucker knew he was right.

At least it wasn't just me. The scent of Hazel was everywhere. All over me and every time I sucked in a breath, she was right there.

"Am I doing this or not?"

Gunnar's lips twitched, the fucker. "I don't know, Saint, are you?"

He cocked a brow my way, daring me to challenge him.

"Damn right, I am. I'll let you know if I see anything worth reporting."

"Anything," Gunnar clarified. "Let me know if you see anything or anyone you don't know or who looks like they don't belong in Opey. I don't want to take no fucking chances. None."

"Got it."

"Good."

His shoulders fell again, proof that this was weighing heavily on him and my respect for Gunnar notched up again. My first impression was that he wanted the cops in his pocket so we could do what the fuck we wanted with no consequences. But I could see now, just how each crime affected him deeply. Especially the one against Terrie.

"All right then. Next we need to talk about what else, fuckin' cattle."

I zoned out at Gunnar's words because though it brought in a shit ton of money for the ranch and the club, I had no interest in cows, cow shit, or how cows became burgers. Holden did just fine with that end of the business, and I had my fill of learning just how a fucking steak was made.

By the time the meeting was over, I was another ball of nerves and half considering another session with Mitch instead of the thing I knew had to be done. And it definitely had to be done.

I had to find a way to convince Hazel to go out with me. Tonight.

For real.

With a hidden agenda she didn't need to know about.

Not yet, anyway.

Chapter Eighteen

Hazel

"You want me to do what?"

Running into my boss and part time lover while I was dressed in nothing but a light blue towel was not my idea of a good time. Sure, my legs trembled at the sight of him in a pair of dark wash jeans and a long sleeve grey shirt that showed off his impressive chest, his thick arms and that tight stomach decorated with a delicious six pack. But that didn't help me understand what the fuck he was talking about.

"You heard me. Go out with me tonight." It wasn't exactly how I expected a guy to act or sound when he asked me out, then again Saint was like no man I'd ever known.

For one thing he didn't bother to even act like he liked me, not even when he wanted to fuck me. If I didn't respect the honesty so much, I might find it loathsome, right along with that deceptively boyish grin he was wearing while my clit throbbed and tried to reach out to him. I was half a second away from jumping on him and riding his face to orgasm, but I couldn't. Not yet.

"Why?"

He scoffed. "What the hell kind of question is that?"

"A good one, I'd say. You barely tolerate me at work and you've already fucked me in every hole imaginable. Why would you ask me out now?"

It didn't make sense, and I learned at an early age to trust my instincts. They were probably the only reason I was still alive.

"I'd like to get to know you, Hazel. I'm not sure I've ever met a woman like you before."

Flattery. Even I wasn't immune to it. "I'm not so special, Saint. I can promise you that."

He stepped closer and ran a finger along the edge of the towel across my chest, making my breath hitch.

"I'd like a chance to decide that for myself. I already know what your incredible mouth can do." His finger traced the line of my lips and I was frozen to the spot, hooked on what he would do next. "I know just how delicious and sweet your pussy is, how juicy she gets when I lick her just so."

One hand slid under the towel and skated over my pussy lips until I gasped.

"How tight she gets when I slide my cock deep into her. How you scream when I make you come."

His finger slid in my pussy just enough to feel that he was there without providing any real relief.

"Now I'd like to get to know the rest of you."

"Why?" I looked up into dark green eyes, deep and intense in their heat as his finger slid deeper and deeper, until he was right where I needed him.

"You can see if I'm what you obviously think I am and maybe you'll convince me you're not as special as you seem. Plus there will be food and booze."

He had me there. "You should've led with that. I can put up with anyone long enough to put away a steak and a beer."

He laughed and it was a good sound, deep and rich and so full of life it was at odds with the darkness Saint wore like a security blanket.

"And you said you were nothing special. I'm calling bullshit."

I rolled my eyes and ignored that warmth that spread throughout my body at his words. I didn't want to be flattered to feel complimented by his words, but I was only human. A weak, weak human.

"What time are we leaving on this last minute date of ours?"

He at least had the grace to blush. "Seven o'clock good?"

"Should I dress like it's a date or do I need to dress to run?"

He hadn't said so yet, and I had a feeling he wouldn't, but I knew Saint was up to something. This date had 'ulterior motives' written all over it, but I was bored and hungry, and the idea of fucking Saint again was worth the effort of getting ready for a date.

"It's a date so dress like it's a date."

I wanted to smack his face at his smart ass remarks, but his commanding tone hit me right between the thighs. If he wanted me to dress for a date, I would blow his fucking mind.

Before the date, and if he was lucky, after.

"You got it. Boss."

He quirked a brow but wisely kept his mouth shut as he turned and walked away. I watched him go until the sight of that denim hugging his ass and thighs was no more.

When Saint was gone, I called the one person who knew me best for advice.

"Jessie, I need help with a date night outfit, and I only have a few things from my house. Think I should go shopping?" I told her with a smile, pulling the phone away from my ear at her squeal of excitement.

Apparently, this was my life now.

Chapter Nineteen

Saint

"Jesus fucking Christ, Hazel. Are you trying to kill me?" The woman knew how to fill out a dress and the one she wore tonight was all white, a sharp contrast to her dark hair and eyes, nearly melting into pale porcelain flesh. The dress was pretty, way feminine with lace all over, giving glimpses of bare skin.

Hazel's lips spread into a slow grin as she shrugged. "Not *kill* you, no. Just dressing for a date. Like you said."

I smiled at her wording. "Wow. Okay."

"Hmm," was her only response. "You want me to change?" She lifted a dark brow at me, daring me.

I stepped in close enough that I could smell the perfume on her skin, the fruity scent of her shampoo. So I could see that little fluttering pulse in her throat, the one that gave her away every single time.

"If you change right now, the only thing I'll be eating for dinner is you."

I smiled at the way she shivered at my words, enjoying the playful banter between us.

"As great as that sounds, I was promised steak, and I really, really can't give it up to a man who breaks his promises."

Her words were playful but I couldn't shake the feeling that there was a hint of truth in those words.

I shrugged and took a step back, waving her towards the front of the bunkhouse.

"You make a better dessert anyway."

"Let's see how juicy the steak is before we start talking dessert, boss man."

She flashed a sexy smile over her shoulder that made my jeans so tight I had to take a long moment walking around the car to get my body under control.

"Nice car," she finally said when I slid behind the wheel and got the car on the road.

"Thanks. It was the first, and only, big purchase I made when I retired from the Army." Retired. That was a fucking joke. They called it a medical discharge but that was just a term to make us feel better about no longer being useful to our government.

Hazel slid her hands over the soft leather seats, the dust-free dashboard and the gearshift with a smile.

"I'm guessing you earned every penny of this baby. Dream car or what?"

My shoulders relaxed as I turned onto the dark two-lane road that went from Hardtail Ranch straight into the heart of Opey proper. I knew Hazel wouldn't ask questions that were hard to answer because she wouldn't want the favor returned.

"Can't say I ever really had a dream car. Growing up in New York isn't the same as most of the country. We're not all eager to get our licenses at sixteen and saving up for our dream car by eighteen." I shrugged again. "I had enough for a significant down payment to keep the monthly payments low, and I liked the color."

Hazel smiled at me like I was the most amusing creature she'd ever encountered, but instead of being put off, I was amused in return.

"Funny, I thought you would've gotten a green car to match your eyes."

I barked out a laugh at that. "Not something men do, sweetheart."

Who in the hell chose a car based on eye color?

"Is that what you did?"

She laughed again. This time it was deep and throaty and sexy as hell.

"Hell no. I chose it because I could afford it, and it had the fewest miles of any other cars in the lot."

It was a practical answer from a practical woman and as much as I appreciated it, I wanted to be the one to show her how to be *im*practical.

"When you were on active duty, did you just have your checks deposited into the bank?"

I nodded, wondering where this line of questioning was headed.

"Yeah. Direct deposit and I only needed it when I was on leave or when I came home. If nothing else, being active military is an excellent savings plan."

Hazel laughed again. "They should use that for the recruitment poster."

I put the car in park and made my way around to the passenger side. She was still chuckling when I opened her door and took her hand. "If nothing else, you'll save a shit ton of money with Uncle Sam."

I couldn't deny that her laugh was contagious, giving me a chance to laugh that I'd denied myself for too long.

"Thanks for that," I told her when her laughter died down. I guided her into Tex's Longhorn Steak House, the best and only steakhouse in all of Opey.

"For what?" Her dark brows pulled together in an adorable frown, and I resisted the urge to kiss the bunched up skin between her brows.

"It's been hard to think of my time in the military with a smile or a laugh."

I didn't know why I admitted that her to except for the fact that Mitch kept insisting that sharing good memories is better than hoarding the bad ones.

She frowned. "Did you not like the Army or was it all the bad shit you saw?"

Again, her questions were genuine and matter of fact, there was none of the sickening *desire* to know all the gory details.

"I loved the service," I told her as we waited to be seated. "The guys in my unit were my best friends, hell they were family to me. Let's just say it was the culmination of a lot of bad shit that ended with my whole family dead."

"Shit, Saint."

Her words were soft, quietly shocked, but instead of trying to make me feel better with trite words and disgusting platitudes, Hazel just wrapped her arms around me.

"Losing people you love sucks donkey balls."

I laughed at the truth of that statement and dropped a kiss on the bottom of her forehead. It was an intimate gesture, far too intimate for our current relationship, but it felt nice. Necessary.

"Damn right it does."

"Saint party for two, your table is ready." The pretty waitress led us to our table and rattled off the specials before leaving us once again.

"So, Saint. Tell me about your friends in the military."

I gave her a look to see if she was being serious, but Hazel's gaze had already gone back to the leather bound menu.

"What do you want to know?"

She shrugged. "Who was the funny one? Which one made sure you guys had girls wherever you went on leave? Who was the gross one who told dirty jokes and crude hookup stories? Tell me."

Shit, I hadn't thought about that in ages. "Jank was the guy in charge, though he didn't act like it until he had to."

The longer I told her about the guys, Higgs and Pony Boy, too, the easier it was to talk.

"Higgs was my best friend. Our driver. The guy could find his way around any city on the globe, and if he couldn't, there was always a person willing to help. Not that Higgs took advantage, but Pony Boy sure did."

Her laugher was music to my wounded soul and I longed to hear more of it over dinner.

"Sounds like my friend Jessie, who's more like my sister. We met in foster care, and we've been friends ever since, but she's a total man magnet. No matter where we went, there was always some hot guy who wanted to open the door for us, show us how to get someplace or buy us a drink. Jessie though? She was oblivious. Thought people were just good and kind in the world because she was."

Hazel shook her head wistfully and I could tell that Jessie, whoever she was, was her family.

"Foster care, huh? Was it as awful as people say?"

Why the fuck did I ask that? Of course it was terrible, and she probably didn't want to talk about it.

"It was worse, actually. But Jessie made it better. Somehow, together, we were able to make it until we aged out and left to our own devices."

She smiled at the memory, but I saw the strain around her eyes as she thought about her friend. "She fell in love with a cowboy and they live in Oklahoma with their three little munchkins."

I raised my glass and she did the same. "To the ones who made it out and lived to tell the tale."

"Cheers to those brave, crazy, lucky souls."

She smiled and knocked her drink back, leaving me no other choice but to watch as the cool amber liquid slid down her throat, and she smacked her lips together in sweet satisfaction.

"Damn, there's just something about whiskey and red meat that go together like bikers and Harleys."

She quirked a knowing brow at me before she burst out laughing.

"You didn't think it was a secret, did you?"

"Not a secret, no. Not exactly." I don't know what the hell I thought about the whole biker thing. It was a natural next step for me, having a family similar to the one I lost, but I still couldn't feel it yet.

"You don't want to talk about it."

It wasn't a question, and she didn't sound upset about it. Not yet, anyway.

"It's not that, but what do I say about it?"

Hazel shrugged. "What's it like? Being a biker?"

"Don't know. This is my first time."

I didn't feel like a constant bad ass or some kind of enforcer, just a guy who happened to be in a motorcycle club.

She laughed again. "You all seem like cool guys, so I guess I'm curious what you do. Are you rich guys who just ride bikes once in a while in matching outfits? Or do you smash heads and protect people from other, worse bad guys?"

Her questions, ridiculous as they were, pulled more laughter from me and after a while the sound was no longer rusty. No longer unfamiliar.

"Do you have a thing for bikers, Hazel?"

"No. I mean other than on TV, I don't know any bikers so I guess I'm just curious about your way of life."

Fair enough. "I guess you could say we protect people, at least we're trying to."

I didn't know how much to tell her because this was club business and she wasn't a Reckless Bastard. Then again, I wondered how much Gunnar told Peaches about what we did. *She's not your woman,* a voice inside of me insisted.

Hazel nodded and got lost in thought for a long moment, making me wonder what was going on in her pretty little head.

"You lead a very interesting life, Saint."

"I wouldn't say that, but it does have its moments."

Like this particular moment right now, it was one I knew I couldn't forget even if I tried. Which I wouldn't. Not ever.

"I've had a nice long moment with this steak, so thank you for that."

She flashed a brilliant million-watt smile that was so damn contagious that when the waitress stopped by with our check, she found me and Hazel staring at each other like two silly teenagers.

"Dessert for you love birds?"

"No thanks," Hazel insisted. "Apparently he wants to lose a game of pool to me before the night is over."

The waitress smiled and shrugged it off before she walked away with a bounce in her step.

"Do I?"

She shrugged. "I don't know Saint, do you?"

***

"This place feels like it should have peanut shells on the floor!"

I should have reconsidered volunteering to be the first one to do recon on the guys in town, but with Hazel's tits and her curves pressed against me, I was happy to be the guinea pig.

"Maybe we're too early for the peanut shells," I whispered in her ear, happy to keep her as close as she was now. "Drink?"

"Trying to get me drunk, boss man?"

"No, smart ass, it's what people do in bars. At least they did when I used to frequent these establishments."

It had been a long time since I'd sat in a bar and shot the shit, even longer since I'd done it with a pretty woman on my arm.

"I think I'll just have a whiskey on the rocks. This place looks like they frown on fancy orders like a Manhattan or an Old Fashioned."

She turned to me with a smile and stepped in closer just as a group of guys entered.

I couldn't say what it was about the guys that put me on alert, only that it did. Two of them were blond-haired cowboys and the third, with the dark hair, looked like he'd done a few years behind bars. They certainly had my attention.

"We can risk it if you want. I'll protect you."

I pulled her in close and Hazel let me, smiling as her hands landed on my chest, roaming all around before they came to a stop at my waistband.

"I'll have a whiskey on the rocks, Saint. That way I can protect you if you need it." That damn cheeky smile on her face just about ripped my heart from my chest. "But I will accept your challenge on the game of pool."

"I don't recall issuing the challenge, but I won't turn down a chance to see you bent over the table, showing off that ass."

And since the other three guys had taken up the table in the corner, it gave me a perfect opportunity to observe them. They were troublemakers, I could see that clearly, based on the loud way they laughed and talked, being intentionally disruptive. They were handsy with the waitresses and any other solitary women unlucky enough to end up in their orbit.

"Men," she scoffed. "So damn easy."

She walked away and I grabbed our drinks, following behind at a safe enough distance to watch and to protect. "How's this table?"

It was perfect. One table separated us from the threesome, just enough to listen carefully without getting involved.

"Perfect," I told her and snapped a few photos over my shoulder to send to the guys if my instincts turned out to be correct. "You want to break first?"

"Hell, no." She threw her head back and laughed, drawing the attention of the younger blond in the threesome. "I'll rely on your masculine strength to break 'em apart, and then I'll wipe the floor with you."

Her confidence was amusing and endearing, so much so, I was half tempted to let her win, but it was unnecessary because she won the first game on her own.

"I guess now it's time for me to get serious."

She laughed, holding the pool cue and unconsciously stroking it. Teasing me. Tempting me beyond all reason. "Guess so."

"Hey baby, what's your name?" The young kid with the curly blond hair had finally found his courage in the bottom of beer number three and was taking his shot.

"The name is Hazel, not *baby*." Her guarded look told him she was not amused, like she was used to dealing with drunken assholes like him.

"Hazel, huh? I like it. So Hazel, why don't you drop this old man and get with a young buck who can keep you up all night?"

Hazel looked at him, assessed everything about him from his height to the size of his muscles, before she reacted. "I'm a one woman man and totally in love with him. Sorry, kiddo."

His nostrils flared the second time she called him kid, and she took a step back. *Good girl.* "All women think that until they've had a real man." He grabbed her by the waist and pulled her close to him before she had a chance to react.

Hazel pushed at his chest and pulled a classic move, smacking him and dragging her nails down the side of his face.

"Get off me, asshole!" He grabbed his face and stumbled back.

"You rotten bitch!"

He lunged for Hazel, but I was already there, right between them, completely unnoticed by this asshole the entire time. I stood between this guy and Hazel, waiting—no *daring*—that asshole to give me a reason to pound him into the fucking ground.

"Watch how you talk to her or your face won't be the only thing fucked up around here, dickhead."

His bodyguards stood behind him, arms crossed and doing a very good impression of two guys who might kick my ass, unless I didn't notice that they stood *behind* that asshole. I bent down and grabbed the punk by the t-shirt.

"Touch my lady again, and I'll beat the smile off your fucking face. Got it?"

He sneered first, not quite sure if he should be afraid of me or not. Like I told the guys, I wasn't immediately intimidating, and I knew assholes like this would take the fucking bait. Hook, line and sinker.

"Fuck you and that dirty bitch of yours."

"You made your choice," I told him and pulled my arm back, letting my fist snap against his nose. "Asshole!"

Blood rushed from his nose and his friends were more concerned about their own faces than helping him.

Hazel tugged me away, and I took several deep breaths before I stopped her or dared look at her. Some women got a kick out of men fighting over them, but I didn't think Hazel was that kind of chick. I also didn't know if the violence would piss her off.

"Come on slugger, let me buy you a drink."

"Slugger?"

She shrugged and smiled at me over her shoulder. "It's not exactly new, but it fits the bill. Beer or something stronger?"

I frowned. "You're not upset?"

She shook her head and leaned across the bar to place our orders before she slid down and pressed close to me.

"No. I mean I hate fighting, but damn, that got me kind of hot."

"Yeah? Tell me more."

Her eyes shone with mischief, and I knew I was in trouble when she leaned in and let her lips brushed my earlobe. "Watching you go caveman on that idiot was so fucking hot, I can't wait to show you—"

That was all I needed to hear before I was off my stool and tugging Hazel behind me, not stopping until I had her outside and her back pressed against the passenger side of my car and me pressed to her front. "Tease."

"Get in the car and find out," she panted, brows arched in a challenge.

I couldn't wait to find out, but the road back to Hardtail was dark and on a moonless night like tonight, dangerous as fuck. The air was silent and tense with desire between us. My hands gripped the steering wheel to avoid reaching out to touch Hazel's creamy legs.

"Hazel," I breathed out a warning when her hand gripped my thigh.

"Yeah?"

"Driving here."

A soft giggle escaped even as her hand continued stroking and massaging my thigh, her pinky brushing against my balls with every move.

"Not preventing you from driving. Just...*exploring*." Her hands explored my thigh from my knee all the way up to my cock and back down again. Then she flipped the button on my jeans, and the zipper came next.

"Hazel."

"Shhh," she urged and leaned forward to swipe her tongue across the head of my dick. "I've been thinking about getting my mouth on you all night and I won't stop until you do. Unless you're worried we'll crash."

With her warning issued, Hazel's mouth wrapped around my cock and made it impossible to focus on the road with my eyes rolling back in my head and my body seizing with pleasure.

"Oh shit, woman!" She took me deep and licked my balls, teasing me when she knew I couldn't do a damn thing about it.

"Fuck, Hazel!" I felt her smile around my cock but she never stopped, licking and sucking me like I was her favorite late night snack and I couldn't even thrust a little.

"Hazel," I warned as my balls tightened and my spine began to tingle.

She took me deep one final time and that was it. I lost my shit as the car came to a stop too damn close to the wall on the side of the bunkhouse. My whole body jerked as I emptied my balls down her throat, and Hazel swallowed every fucking drop.

My legs were shaky as I stepped from the car, but after a blowjob like that, a man had only one fucking thing on his mind. Fucking. A good hard punishing fuck for the beautiful, magnificent woman who'd given it to him.

"What are you—?"

I cut off Hazel's words when I yanked her from the car and tossed her over my shoulder. I locked us up in the bunkhouse and laid her on the first empty bed I found. And that was where I kept her, feasting on her body until the sun came up.

Chapter Twenty

Hazel

I couldn't remember the last time I'd woken up with a smile on my face. It was a novelty for sure, and I let myself revel in it for a moment. Okay, a *long* moment. The muscles in my thighs ached, ab muscles I didn't realize I had pinched with every little intake of breath, and I relished it all as erotic flashes of the night before came to me. I reached out beside me for the man who'd given me so much pleasure, but he wasn't there.

Saint was gone. No, not just gone, the bed was cold which meant he'd been gone for a long time. Probably not long after I fell asleep if history was any indication.

Not that I blamed him. The beds on this side of the bunkhouse were tiny as fuck, twin size beds. When I drifted off to sleep half of me was on top of his hard, lean body. Even though I understood why he left, when I sat s up and scanned the empty room and saw no trace of him, not a stray sock or forgotten boxer shorts, I felt empty and disappointed. Discarded.

Which was stupid. Saint didn't owe me anything but the pleasure he'd spent the night lavishing on me, and that was plenty. More than plenty, in fact. It wasn't like he was my boyfriend or anything.

Although he did call me his lady to those punks at the bar. Probably just to protect me.

At least that was what I told myself as I slid from the bed, ignoring the evidence of our sexual gymnastics as I made my way to the bathroom for a long hot shower. It wasn't long enough to make me forget last night or hot enough to completely rinse away his scent. But, it was long enough to remind me why sleeping with my boss was a bad fucking idea, no matter how good the sex made me feel.

Dressed in jeans and a plain black tank top, I stepped into my favorite black sneakers, packed my bags and drove into Opey. The town was a nice, idealized television version of a small town. Instead of paved or cobbled streets and sidewalks, it had beautifully painted and stained wooden slats. All of the little businesses had cute little awnings with kitschy names and funky logos that never failed to put a smile on my face. The few businesses boarded up thanks to the recent rash of robberies cast the only dark spots on the town.

This crime spree didn't make any sense to me. Opey had its bad apples like every place does. Farm boys who liked to fight after a few too many beers and left the wrong girls brokenhearted, but not homegrown criminals. They didn't beat up old ladies and they sure as hell didn't start fires. I had an uneasy feeling these crimes were the beginning of something bigger.

The police had taken the tape down from the front of Edna Mae's place even though she had to remain in the hospital for a few more days. At least, that's what I'd heard from the grapevine. The lack of police tape gave me hope that I could get inside my apartment, so I walked around the building, strolling really, just in case someone had their eyes on me. I kept my fingers crossed.

The tape was scattered on the ground in shreds that didn't look too official, but I went inside anyway. It was my apartment, and I had to pay rent on it whether I lived inside or not. I preferred to live inside, especially when my only other option was sharing living quarters with a man I wanted more than I wanted normal.

I couldn't stop thinking about the whole situation with Saint, not when I went back downstairs to grab my bags from the car, and not as I began the time-consuming task of cleaning my apartment. The robbers, whoever they were, had left my place a mess. The police hadn't doubled their efforts trying to collect any evidence they could. Fingerprint dust covered nearly every surface of my living room and bedroom, and black fingerprints covered most of my kitchen.

A fucking mess.

I pulled out my yellow cleaning bucket and all the supplies I'd gotten from a dollar store in town and got to work. I never found comfort or solace in cleaning. I knew Jessie did, though. It had always been a necessary evil in my life, required by foster families first and then later it was a good way to keep from overstaying my welcome on somebody else's couch. But now, I cleaned to get rid of the intruders. I cleaned because my mind wouldn't stop thinking and worrying and analyzing. "More like *over*analyzing." And it was all Saint's fault.

What the hell was I doing with him anyway? The last thing I needed was someone as fucked in the head as me, maybe more fucked. And he was my boss. Still, I wanted him. There was something about Saint that called out to me. Made me want to reach out and take his hand instead of letting him run away. Which was a stupid fucking thought to have about a vet who clearly had PTSD but was now mixed up with a motorcycle gang—and the manager of a full blown sex club.

Knowing all that, I still wanted him with an intensity I couldn't describe or understand. All I knew was that I wanted him and I shouldn't. Couldn't.

There was one person I could call who would understand and offer advice. With a smile, I dialed her number.

"Hey Haze, what's up?"

I smiled as I always did at the sound of Jessie's voice. These days she was always in a hurry, either running after kids or cattle, or shuffling them from one activity to the next. "Is this a good time to talk?"

"Is it ever?"

I could hear the smile in her voice, and if I closed my eyes, I could see her shaking her head, long hair brushing her shoulders.

"No, but you're my person I call when I need to talk."

"Kids are quiet. What's up, girl?"

I sucked in a deep breath and told her about Saint. "He asked me out on a date and it was a great date, Jess. But it was a last minute thing, which makes me wonder what the real reason was."

I told her about waking up alone and being disappointed. "I'm fucked, aren't I?"

Jessie was quiet for a long moment before she laughed. "Pretty much, I'm afraid. Is he good? Does he treat you right?"

"He is good, Jessie. But he's screwed up, too. I don't know if it's his screwed up-ness calling out to me, or if it's him, as a person."

If anyone understood, it was Jessie. She'd been there for everything.

"The fact that you're worried about it tells me it's him you like. Not his problems."

"I know," I told her impatiently.

"Just sayin'," she said in a sing-song voice that usually made me want to strangle her. Today I just wished she was close enough to hug.

"Shit, hang on!" The phone went silent for a long time and then Jessie was back.

"Sorry Haze, I've gotta go before my kids electrocute themselves and knock out the power, but listen, give this a chance. You could get hurt or you could hurt him. Either way, I love you and there's always Oklahoma."

I rolled my eyes. "If you love me, why would you wish Oklahoma on me? That's not love, girl."

She laughed. "Because it's where your family is, dummy. Hey! Gotta go. Love ya!"

She ended the call before I could say it back, which was just as well anyway. Jessie's life was busy, most days too busy for anything but tending to her family and the ranch. I needed to get used to leaning on myself more. That meant I needed to save money and to do that, I needed to keep my job.

Another strike against Saint.

But once I was in the shower, washing hours of dust and muck from my skin, all I could think about was how Saint felt with his warm body pressed against mine, his cock invading my body, his hands making me purr like a kitten. When I closed my eyes and saw his smile, that dark intensity that always gripped him during sex, all I wanted was him. Consequences be damned.

It didn't stop me from making myself come in the shower with images of his tongue deep inside my pussy. It probably wouldn't stop me from finger fucking myself to thoughts of him again later. For now, I grabbed the latest romantic thriller I'd got from the public library and curled up in bed with an aluminum bat at my side.

Halfway through the second chapter a knock sounded at the door. I reached for the bat, ignoring my need to cover up my body for whoever was on the other side of the door, because they wouldn't be getting inside. I tiptoed to the door and peeked through the peephole. It was Saint. I pulled the door open and gave him my best bored look.

"Saint. What are you doing here?"

"You left," he growled and barged in, kicking the door shut behind him.

KB Winters

Chapter Twenty-One

Saint

Hazel stood there with a bored as hell look on her face, one hand wrapped tightly around a baseball bat.

"You left first."

"I did." My gaze roamed over her rainbow-striped tank top that hugged her tits and her small waist, nipples hard through the little strips of white between each color, and as my gaze slid lower to the strip of skin revealed before the tiniest goddamn scrap of fabric I had ever seen, my cock stirred.

"I had some business that couldn't wait, and I hoped to come back, maybe pick up where we left off. But you were gone."

And I had to find a way to stop my dick from trying to bust out of my jeans on the drive to town.

She shrugged, rolling her dark eyes as if it didn't matter. As if none of it mattered. Then again, maybe it didn't matter to her. Maybe one dirty fuck was as good as another.

"That was hours ago. Must have been important business."

Her tone said she didn't think it was, that she thought I was full of shit.

"You didn't need to come down here to check on me, Saint. You didn't make me any promises, and I'm not upset. Looks like my place was cleared by the cops so I'm home now."

Was she out of her mind? I shook my head and ran my fingers through my hair before I said something to piss her off.

"It hasn't been cleared. If it had, the police would have told you. Plus, those guys are still out there and in case you didn't notice, they didn't finish ransacking your place."

I knew I scared her with those words but dammit, she needed to see reason.

"What makes you say that?"

"Because I'm not an idiot, Hazel. You and Peaches came back here to get whatever you were worried about. She told Gunnar so don't deny it."

"I don't need to deny anything since I don't owe you an explanation."

My lips spread into a slow grin at her angry tone. Goddamn Hazel was tough, but right now she was also being stupid.

"No, you don't owe me an explanation, but chances are, these guys are gonna come back here to see if they missed anything. I'd rather you not be here when they do."

Cruz and Slayer were on patrol tonight but these guys were good at staying invisible.

"I can take care of myself."

"Of that, I have no doubt, babe."

She glared at the endearment, which only made me laugh. And push in closer.

"What were you gonna do with that bat?"

"Kick your ass."

She wore her best tough girl look. I took another step forward.

"You really think you can?" My lips quirked up in a grin.

Her dark eyes gave an expert roll but she took one step back and then another.

"Yeah, probably not. So, what? Are you here for another round?"

"No, that's not why I'm here. Not yet, anyway."

Sparring with Hazel was some of the best parts of my day and I didn't even want to think about what fresh hell that meant. Though I was sure Mitch would have a field day with it, if I told him.

"We've been monitoring the situation in town with the robberies, the fire, all of it. We think we know who they are, and we're trying to track them down."

Even that was too much, but I knew telling her nothing wouldn't get her to do what I wanted her to do.

"*We* as in your gang?"

"Club, but yes."

She snorted and rolled her eyes, a move that might've been annoying if she weren't damn near naked.

"Bikers with a heart of gold?"

Her sarcasm was palpable, and I tried hard not to be offended.

"Don't be so bitchy just 'cause you're scared, babe."

She glared even harder, and I my smile grew wide.

"Look this is serious shit, Haze. What do you think they'll do to you if they break in and find you like this? Because I can tell you what I'd like to do to you right now."

Her eyes lit with challenge. "Tell me."

"I'm being serious."

"Me too."

She placed her hand on her hip but she never set the bat down. "Tell me what you want to do to me, right now, and I'll listen to what you have to say. I promise."

"First, you need to drop the bat. Then, I'll peel that tank top off and wrap my lips around those nipples that've been aching for my mouth since you opened the door. I'd lick and suck those gorgeous tits until you arched into me with that sexy mewling cry you do, until I could smell your arousal in the air around us, and then I'd keep sucking until you came."

She swallowed with a nod; her eyes now darker with desire.

"And then?"

My dirty girl wanted more, and I was happy to give it to her.

"Then I'd push you down onto that chair right there and put your ankles by your ears, lapping up all the juices dripping down your leg, coating your pussy lips. I'd lick it all up until you were a hot, trembling mess and then I'd let you fuck my mouth until you came again."

She let out a shuddering breath that told me she liked what she heard, before slicking that pink tongue across her bottom lip.

"Good to know," she said, trying her damnedest to appear unaffected and failing miserably.

"You sure you don't want to know what I have in mind for that pretty ass of yours?"

"Not if you ever want to say what you came here to say."

Her honesty pulled a laugh out of me.

"Right." Damn woman knew how to twist me up good. "These guys are reckless and dangerous, with a violent streak. The crimes, as far as we can tell, are mostly for fun. Nothing major is stolen just enough cash to party with for a few days."

That meant there were no stakes other than what they created and soon, they would up the stakes of these crimes. It was a story I'd seen and heard in the military time and again, on both sides of the war.

"Shit, you really have been tracking this." With a nervous, half-absent nod, Hazel scanned her apartment. "You really think I'm in danger?"

"We'd already be fucking if I didn't."

I hoped she could see the truth of my words because if she waited any longer, we'd be fucking anyway.

"Right. Let me grab some stuff." She set the bat down as she brushed past me. "You know who these guys are?"

"We have an idea."

"And what do you plan to do about it?"

From another woman the question might have sounded prodding, but I knew she was just curious. I didn't know how I knew, but I did.

"That's the part we're trying to figure out. Gunnar wants to teach them a hard to forget lesson and most of the guys agree, but Holden agrees with me that prison would be just as satisfying."

"Please try not to kill anyone in my apartment, or else I won't get my deposit back." She appeared in the doorway of her bedroom dressed in jeans and a white t-shirt with a very red bra underneath and biker boots on her feet. "I could use that money."

"Going somewhere?"

She shrugged. "Not now, but I find it's best to always be ready to hit the road."

To prove it, she had two medium sized duffel bags all packed and ready to go.

"That's it?"

"It's everything I need. We ready? I gotta work tonight and sometimes my boss can be a real asshole."

I laughed and grabbed one of the bags from her, expecting a protest but she put up none. "It's probably how he keeps you in line."

She snorted and pulled open the door, motioning for me to go out ahead of her.

"In his dreams."

"Wanna hear about those?" I leaned in and whispered the words in her ear while she locked the door and that little intake of breath sent a sliver of desire straight to my cock.

"Maybe later."

We had a long night ahead of us so I wasn't worried at all.

***

"You guys really went all out for this theme."

It wasn't the first time Hazel had said those words, but now we were alone and I had the time and interest.

"Gunnar liked the idea and the members seem to love it."

Not that I was all that surprised since I pitched the idea, telling him that these rich Texans saw themselves as modern day Romans so the excesses and indulgences felt like their due.

"What do you think?"

"It looks incredible, just like walking on the set of Spartacus. Complete with oiled up sex slaves."

Her teasing tone and her eyes full of desire told me she'd enjoyed it as much as every other woman tonight.

"It was a good idea."

"Who said it was my idea?"

"Right." She shook her head and rolled her eyes before turning away to scan the last of the room for glasses, straws and other debris forgotten about when the mood struck.

"Well it was an inspired idea."

Without another word she brushed past me and hustled out the door.

It took me a moment to realize she'd left, and I scrambled after her. "Hazel, wait!"

But the hall was empty. "Hazel?"

Logically, I knew she had to be somewhere, here, on the sub level with me. She couldn't have gotten upstairs that quickly. "Hazel?"

She wasn't in the water room or the wine room.

Or the dining room.

"Hazel!"

That left the forest room.

I stepped inside the dimly lit space, done up mostly in dark greens and browns with matching blankets nestled on the ground for ultimate member comfort. Panic rose up in my throat, and I couldn't explain the sudden urgency to find Hazel. "Hazel, where are you?"

"I'm here, Saint."

I heard her voice, but it was too goddamn dark, and I couldn't see. Combined with the nascent background sounds, my chest began to pound and my hearing grew muffled. Shit, I knew what this was and my eyes slammed shut.

"Saint. Come here. Come to me."

I heard her voice, but I couldn't figure out where it was coming from. The moment I opened my eyes, I wasn't inside one of the rooms of The Barn Door, I was back in the goddamn desert. The sun was too fucking bright, making it difficult to see and heat emanated from every surface, at least a hundred and fifteen degrees.

"Saint!"

"Hazel! I'm coming!" I shouted out.

At least I would be when the smoke cleared. Where the fuck was all this smoke coming from anyway? Everything was all mixed up, and I needed to get the fuck out of there. Fast.

"Saint?"

My name came softer from her lips. Closer, too. And then a hand was on my shoulder, and I spun around, grabbing the throat of whoever was behind me and pushing that fucker against a wall.

"Saint, it's me. Hazel."

Hazel? Her words were soft but I heard the edge of panic in them, even though it wasn't Hazel in front of me. It was a nameless, faceless body.

"What do you want? Answer me!"

"Saint, it's me. It's Hazel."

"What do you want?"

"You," she choked out, literally. "I want you, Saint."

Soft, feminine hands cradled my face. "Look at me."

"I...can't." If I opened my eyes and Hazel was in the desert with me, then it meant this wasn't a dream. That it was all real.

"You can. Look at me. Now."

To punctuate the words, she slapped my face, hard.

"The fuck?"

My eyes were open now. "Why did you do that?"

She shrugged. "You needed it."

I took a step back, and she reached out to me, looking hurt when I stepped out of her reach.

"I can't do this, not now."

"Seems like you can to me."

She bridged the distance between us and wrapped her hand around my cock, squeezing until I groaned.

"But you're not in the mood and that's fine. Have a good night, Saint."

The fact that she could walk away so easily pissed me off, or maybe it was being in the middle of a pretty fucking big meltdown where I didn't know if I was in the Middle East or Hardtail Ranch.

"Wait."

"Nope, see you tomorrow." She waved and my feet were on the move, right on her ass.

"I. Said. Wait."

My words came out on a growl in her ear, my arm wrapped around her waist and lifted her in the air, tugging her back into the room.

"I heard you."

Scanning the room, my heart still racing, I found the perfect spot to inflict a little erotic punishment on Hazel. And my demons.

"You said you want me. Did you mean it?"

She nodded, eyes wide and filled with desire but there was a hint of fear that worried me. Excited me.

"I can't hear you."

"Yes, I meant it."

My lips quirked at her obedience. "I like this version of you. She's very…good."

Hazel snorted as I set her down in front of a façade wall with shackles at three different heights. "Not too good, I hope."

She was breathless and even in the dim light of the room I could see her flushed skin.

"That depends. Tell me to stop and I will."

When she said nothing, I stripped Hazel out of the thin white wrap she wore and the tiny scrap of hot pink lace, leaving her in nothing but gold stilettos that made my cock hard just thinking of the possibilities. She said nothing when I shackled her arms to the wall or when I dropped to my knees in front of her.

In an act of defiance I should have expected, she crossed her legs at the ankles, concealing that plump pink pussy from me.

"I will."

That was good enough for me, and I grabbed her knees, yanking her legs apart and burying my face in the sweet heat of her pussy. Hazel moaned as I licked and sucked her pussy, nibbled the sensitive flesh of her pussy lips until her legs quivered. It wasn't a gentle move, and I wasn't in a gentle kind of mood, not with my demons breathing down my fucking neck.

"Oh, fuck!"

I smiled against her, still licking. Still sucking her swollen clit, knowing with her arms shackled there was no place to go, she had to take the overload of pleasure. And I fucking overloaded her, feeling my entire face coated with the signs of her pleasure. I sucked her clit until she came. I fucked her with my tongue until she came.

"Saint, please," she panted as I slid two fingers deep inside her pulsing cunt, pulling another gushing orgasm from her.

She shook violently against me as I stood and pulled my cock out of my pants.

"Please, what?"

"More."

With Hazel's arms still out of commission, I lifted one leg and slid in deep on a groan.

"Fucking hell!" She was so goddamn wet I was pretty sure a premature load was on its way out.

"More. Harder."

Her voice was serious, strained but serious and her dark eyes pleaded for more.

"No." I hated the way the demons rose up at her plea, at the need in her eyes and her voice, the greedy way she wrapped herself around my cock.

"Please, Saint. I need it."

Give it to her, the voice urged. *You both want it.*

"You want more?"

"Give it to me," she said instead of answering.

In one quick move her arms were free, and I had Hazel face down on the ground, a chenille blanket buried under her for comfort, both hands behind her back with my hand clenched around her wrists.

"Tell me to stop."

"Don't. Stop."

"Tease," I growled and tightened my grip on her wrists.

"Up."

At the command, her ass lifted in the air, giving me a perfect view from behind.

"Your pussy is so fucking swollen and wet. Perfect."

She wiggled, and I couldn't resist leaning down for a small taste. And then another taste at the bundle of nerves between her sweet cheeks.

"Fuck!"

Hazel wiggled again, this time adding a greedy moan and shot straight to my cock. I stroked it twice and slid him deep inside her wet, pulsing cunt.

"Oh shit." She was hot and wet and pulsing around me like a motorized fucking pussy. "Hazel."

"More."

With my free hand I gripped her hips, squeezing her wrists hard enough that I knew she'd have bruises tomorrow, but as I pounded in the heaven of her pussy, I didn't give a shit. Buried deep in the wet heat, the memories remained at bay. Just out of reach with something far more enticing closer. *Hazel.* With every thrust she collided against me, moaning and crying and—still—begging for more. Those needy little cries had my cock as hard as he'd ever been, and I wasn't ready for this to be over.

Not yet.

With her hands now loose over her head and my body covering hers, I slid in and out in rough, deep thrusts.

"Yes! Fuck, Saint, yes!"

"You like it rough," I growled in her ear, giving her the hard as fuck thrusts she craved, feeling gratitude with every pulse of her inner walls.

"Oh fuck," she moaned, long and loud as an orgasm erupted out of her but I didn't stop. I couldn't.

I pulled out and flipped her over so I could see those dark, tortured eyes while I made her come again.

"Good?"

"Great." Her hand snaked between us and stroked my cock, slick with her own juices, and she smiled.

"Better than."

"Good to know," I panted with a smile, but I was still hungry and the demon was nipping at my...heels, "fuck!"

She rubbed the tip of my cock against her pussy to wet it and then slid it to the darker, tighter opening between her ass cheeks.

"You want?"

I nodded like a goddamn fool, and slowly she guided me inside. "Oh. Fuck."

Those moans and pants, the way she took charge of her pleasure and mine had my cock leaking already, and I started to push inside. She was tight as fuck, which said she didn't do this regularly and that only added another layer of how I felt about her.

"Hazel."

"Fuck it, Saint. I need you to. Fuck my ass."

Do it, the demon urged and damned me to hell, because I took everything she offered, got lost in losing myself in her body, in the sensation of being enveloped by her. The way her gold heels dug into my side, that bit of pain only heightened everything. When Hazel's fingers began to play with her clit as her back arched, I was lost.

I was more than lost, I was in trouble.

"Hazel," I growled in warning, the way her asshole pulsed brought me closer to the edge.

"Let go Saint, I'm close." She grabbed one of my wrists and put my hand to her throat, silently begging me to give her what she wanted.

Weak fucker that I was, I gave it to her. Gripping her neck, squeezing that delicate flesh as I fucked her ass turned me on, made my dick even harder as I plunged in and out of her, which got a steady stream of lubrication from her dripping pussy.

"Hazel, oh fuck!" I pounded harder and faster, squeezing her neck with more pressure than was necessary, but as pleasure took over I couldn't stop.

Couldn't control it.

And worse, I didn't want to. I slid in and out until every drop of me was gone, hard and fast, while she kept a tight grip on my wrist with one hand and her clit with the other. She was close, I could feel it as I slid two fingers into her pussy.

"Yes, oh God yes, Saint!" And then, like some kind of goddess of debauchery and kink, she flew apart, dark eyes wide with wonder and for the first time since I met her, genuine happiness.

I'd done that to her. It was just an orgasm, but it felt like more. So I watched as she rode the waves of pleasure, unashamed of her needs, her desires, in fact she reveled in them, laughing as the last of her orgasm slipped away.

"You're beautiful when you come."

She flashed a sleep, satisfied smiled. "You're beautiful when I come too."

I watched her face for a few minutes and then got us both back to the bunkhouse and into one bed.

Where we both belonged.

Chapter Twenty-Two

Hazel

I woke up in an unfamiliar bed and not knowing how I got there, but the delicious aches all over my body were a pretty good indication that I'd had some spectacular sex. The smile on my face was absolute proof of that because so rarely had sex ever made me smile. Cringe. Squirm. Come even, but rarely a smile. I closed my eyes to recall the memories, stretching my muscles and hitting a hard surface that made me jump.

"Shit, you scared the hell out of me, Saint."

"Expecting someone else?"

"Honestly I was expecting no one at all."

I figured he'd be in his own bed and me in mine, but now I could see that the pillowcase under my hair was his and so were the sheets. This was Saint's bed.

"Sorry to disappoint."

"I'm not disappointed at all, just surprised." But now that I was awake and he was awake, naked with all those muscles and tattoos on display. Making my mouth water.

"Since you're here, we should say 'good morning' the right way." My hand slid below the sheet, finding Saint just the way I liked him, hard and ready.

"I like the way you think, Hazel." He pulled me on top of him and fitted his lips to mine, amazingly like they were always meant to be there. Like we were made for each other.

No thoughts like that, I had to remind myself. This was sex. It was fun. That was it. Nothing more.

Yet when my legs parted and I felt the hard ridge of him press against my clit, it felt like it was more. It felt real. Not that I had any fucking clue what real felt like, only that *this* felt different. Somehow.

We kissed like horny teenagers, eager and excited to touch each other but content to simply kiss. It was so simple that I waited, expecting something to happen, to ruin it all.

Saint pulled back with a smile and a groan. "You're trying to kill me, woman."

"Maybe. Or maybe I'm just trying to avoid this awkward conversation we're about to have."

"Awkward?"

"Yep," she nodded. "The one where you tell me that it was fun and amazing and all that, but it can't happen. You're my boss, blah blah. Right?"

I'd heard the story in all its versions, a million times. Knew it by heart, in fact.

"Wrong. I just wanted to say that maybe we ought to be careful at work, in case anyone gets the wrong idea."

"What's that, you like to fuck the help?"

"Seriously? Is that what you're gonna do now, start a fight?"

"No," my shoulders sank. "This is weird and I don't know why, because it shouldn't be."

I hated all these disgusting emotions; it was one of the reasons I kept sex dirty and anonymous.

"It's weird because it matters. You can pretend it doesn't, and I can too, but apparently it does."

His arms wrapped around me from behind and he held me close, warm breath fanning my shoulder.

"I don't know what's going on either Hazel, but I'm done trying to fight it."

That sounded nice but unrealistic. "Easy for you to say. If things end, you'll still have a job."

"So will you."

I snorted because we both knew that was complete bullshit. "You will, I promise you and if you don't believe me, believe Gunnar."

"I don't know, Saint."

"Me either and that's the beauty of it. Let's just move forward and see what happens. Maybe you'll fall in love with me, maybe you'll kill me or maybe we'll end up good friends."

"Good friends who fuck?"

His lips tugged into a smile at my words.

"Nothing wrong with that, right?"

"Right," I agreed and turned in his arms to receive his kiss. It was hot right off the bat, scorching as his hands roamed all over my body while my hands did the same. We were hungry for each other. Again. Or was it still? I didn't know, all I knew was that nothing existed in that moment other than me and Saint.

Until a commotion sounded outside. Voices. A lot of voices that sounded angry. Frantic.

Scared.

"You hear that?"

"Yeah," Saint growled and sat up. In less than a minute he was fully dressed and heading out of the bunkhouse, with me on his tail in slightly less clothing.

"What's going on?" Saint asked.

Gunnar stood in the middle of the group with a thunderous expression on his face.

"Those motherfuckers broke into the club." He looked like a furious king, angry blue eyes blazing wildly as he spoke of revenge and justice. "I'm done playing games with these assholes."

"We're with you," Wheeler agreed with a nod.

"No more fucking around. This time there will be no threats and no second chances. This means war."

Never had three words scared me down to my soul before.

***

"Are we seriously gonna be the women in the kitchen when shit is going down?" I asked.

After all the commotion at dawn and the anger and threats of bodily harm, Saint and Gunnar and the rest of the guys hopped on their four wheelers and hauled ass over to The Barn Door. More than anything, I wanted to go over there just to see what kind of damage these guys could do, but first Saint and then Gunnar *and* Slayer had impressed upon me the importance of staying at the main house. With Peaches and Maisie.

And Glock.

Peaches looked at me with one eyebrow arched so dramatically it was hard not to laugh.

"I don't know about you but I haven't eaten and there's a hungry little girl in the living room who's expecting breakfast. Or brunch, hell some kind of meal and this is it. Gunnar rightly sent Martha and the twin terrors home so it's just us."

Just us. That was a novelty for me, being part of a group, no matter how ragtag or how big a misfit the group was, but Peaches had made it crystal clear that the main house was where I belonged.

"So shut the hell up and get to choppin'?"

She laughed with a shrug. "Pretty much. Besides, having something to do will keep you from worrying about whatever it is our boys are getting up to on the other side of the property."

Our boys.

"Saint isn't my anything."

He was my sometimes lover and that was it. Oh and my boss, but that was definitely it. Nothing more.

"Tell that lie to someone else, sister."

She pointed her knife at me, laughing hysterically like I was the funniest thing since Kevin Hart.

"He's your boy. Your man. Your lover. And my guess, based on the way his eyes bore into you when he said goodbye, your something more."

"There is no more to be. I'm screwed up and he's even more screwed up, that's a recipe for disaster if there ever was one."

And I prided myself on being able to see where a relationship was headed so I could get out long before the bitter end. This thing with Saint had an expiration date, we just didn't know when.

"There's always more. Gunnar hated my guts, until he didn't. And now look at us."

I rolled my eyes. "Hardly the same. Anyway, why are we talking about this? Saint, Gunnar, and all the rest of them are perfectly capable of handling themselves."

That much I was sure about. The rest was pretty murky. "Any idea what these robberies are all about?"

"My guess is a bunch of shit starters blowing through town. Gunnar is convinced it's something more."

Peaches went back to chopping, and I watched her for a long minute, her confident moves around the kitchen seemed to ooze sex appeal. I wondered if she had to practice that or if it came naturally.

"You really think Saint is too screwed up for you?"

Absolutely not. "No, it's not that. I think we're too screwed up for each other. We both have issues, and neither of us is rushing to handle them maturely."

"Or," she said dramatically until she had my full attention. "Maybe it takes the love of the right person to make you *want* to be better."

I snorted. "That's a nice thought, but I can't afford to think like that. Last time I did, I lost everything."

And I had no intentions on doing that ever again, no matter how many promises Saint made.

Peaches gave me a long, slow look, studying me, probably trying to figure out what Saint saw in such a freak. There was no judgement in her eyes, but there was some kind of knowledge that made me uncomfortable.

"Everything is always fucked up Hazel, until it isn't."

"Or it just stays fucked up and never changes," I shot back.

Just because she was in love and everything was right with the world *for her,* didn't mean everyone was that lucky.

"Well with that attitude, it definitely will."

Her lips twitched playfully, and I knew she was fucking with me. "Sorry but that was too damn easy. Seriously though, don't dismiss Saint because of his PTSD. He came by it honestly, and he's been seeing Mitch about it recently."

"Really?" That was news to me, though I didn't know why I was so surprised. It wasn't like I was Saint's real girlfriend and he'd give me his intimate details as pillow talk.

"Good for him."

"Maybe you had something to do with that."

Her hopeful expression was adorable and it reminded me of Jessie, but I had to bark out a laugh at the ridiculousness of her words.

"I didn't. Trust me." Despite his promises, I knew Saint and I were working on borrowed time. One day soon he'd either fuck it up by lying to me or fucking someone else, or he'd get sick of me and my kinks. Maybe he would just grow apart from me and find someone more suitable. Either way, our thing, whatever it was called had a clock ticking. No matter how much I wished otherwise.

"You are one stubborn ass woman, a trait I normally appreciate, but you are damn frustrating. You two are fucking and practically living together, and the look he gave you before following my man into battle, well shit, even my panties were a little wet. Stop ignoring it, and stop being so fucking afraid."

"Oh, I'm sorry, were you waiting for me to deny the fear?" I scoffed. "Every time I trusted a person, I ended up regretting it. My best friend Jessie is the only one who's never let me down."

"Yeah me, too. Vivi, remember?"

How could I forget. "Look Peaches, I appreciate what you're trying to do. Under normal circumstances I'd be all aboard this crazy ass train, but I can't. This is a good job with excellent tips that allows me to put a lot of money away for a rainy day. I can't afford to get fired when he gets tired of fucking me."

"So make sure he doesn't get tired of it."

It was so simple for her and I envied that.

"It's not that simple. I have certain...*needs* that aren't sustainable in the long run for everyone."

"Now I'm intrigued but keep it down because Maisie has wandering ears. That little girl can hear a juicy secret from half a mile away."

The affection I heard in her voice was clear as day, and I hoped she always thought of her man and the little girl that way.

"I'm not giving you details, Peaches. Let's just say I'm what some might consider high maintenance, and I have a feeling what Saint needs is easy. Uncomplicated."

She snorted. "Bullshit. If any of these guys wanted the simple life they would have taken their money from the government and opened up a bike shop or some kind of fucking store, not an MC. And definitely not a sex club. This is where you come when you've been so immersed in the dirt, in the shit and the muck, that it's all you're suited to do."

That made a twisted kind of sense, but that didn't mean that Saint and I had a future. And no matter how much my heart twisted and leapt with hope, I refused to give in to that traitorous bitch. Hope. What a fucking joke.

"I appreciate the advice, but maybe you're just blinded by love."

"Maybe, but that doesn't make me wrong. Saint jumped on the chance to take you out when Gunnar needed someone to do recon and try to ID these guys, and that's straight from Gunnar."

I knew it! Even though my first instinct was to feign outrage, I wasn't all that surprised that our first and only date had taken place under false pretenses.

"Now that's the first thing you've said that makes any kind of sense. Saint didn't *want* to ask me out, he wanted to fuck me and his biker gang homework gave him the perfect pretext."

"You're not seriously mad, are you?"

"Nope." I wasn't, not really. But this time I was disappointed to be right.

Chapter Twenty-Three

Saint

The club was a fucking wreck. A literal fucking wreck with broken glass everywhere, chairs and stools splintered into thousands of pieces, shrapnel stuck in the carpet and even the walls.

"These motherfuckers are dead!"

It was an unusual display of emotion for me, but the looks of anger mixed with sympathy the guys kept sending my way said they understood what this place meant to me. I built this from the ground up.

"They destroyed almost everything."

"Assholes," Gunnar grunted. He was a man of few words, but over the past year I'd learned a lot about him. Gunnar never used ten words when three would suffice. His gaze landed on mine.

"I don't give a fuck about the money, Saint. Fixing this place up is a tax write-off and a drop in the can financially. But this, this is about the fucking principle of this shit, right here. *They* have to answer for what they've done, goddammit."

His anger took over, and I knew it matched what the rest of us were feeling too.

"They violated us," Holden said, his deep baritone low and slow, dipped in steel. The lone cowboy among us took shit like property even more seriously than the rest of us.

"Fuck that," I said, anger making me brave or maybe it was reckless. "They disrespected our business, our MC. Now those motherfuckers gotta pay."

I'd never personally succumbed to bloodlust, not even when I pumped round after round into those desert dwellers who killed my buddies, but I had a healthy respect for the healing power of vengeance.

"Holy shit guys, look who woke up and joined the party!"

Cruz, the funny fucker, slapped me on the back, teasing but it was all good-natured.

"I guess now that he's got a pretty little *chica* to protect, his balls have dropped and he's back in the game."

Everyone laughed, even me, because it was the only thing I could do that wouldn't land me behind bars.

That, and clean. We spent hours getting rid of all the broken furniture and pool sticks, the sex toys that had to be trashed and the lights we had to replace. Every fucking thing that I'd worked so hard on, along with Gunnar, to turn The Barn Door into the premier sex club in Texas, and they fucking tore it apart in an hour.

It gutted me to see months of hard work fucked up by some fucking hoodlums with nothing better to do than take shit from hard working people. Now that they'd fucked with the Reckless Bastards, I was fully on board with making sure they regretted it.

"Well, the good news is that the safe is untouched. Doesn't look like those fuckers were even able to find it."

Wheeler stood at the top of the staircase with arms folded over his massive chest, blue eyes sparkling with something like mischief.

"The better news is that the Sin Room is untouched too. Not for a lack of trying though, fucking idiots."

He wore a smug smile because Wheeler had been the one to suggest enhanced security leading to our inner sanctum.

"Thank God for small fucking favors," Gunnar grunted and swiped a thick hand across his sweaty forehead. "I can't wait to get my hands on these fuckers. Even one of them, one little fucking neck to break."

"Soon man."

Slayer wore his trademark grin but his dark eyes were serious like they so rarely were, and I knew even he meant business.

"Not fuckin' soon enough," Gunnar grunted and tossed more debris into the trash.

WICKED

"I, uh, got somethin' for you, Boss." Ford, one of the younger guys on the team, stood at the main entrance to the club looking green and nervous, but I guess I'd look the same if there was a security breach on my watch.

"Come on in, kid."

Ford walked into the bar, his baby face at odds with the cornfed cowboy look he had going on, hair still Army short. His small beard the only concession he'd made to civilian life so far. He set the laptop on the bar, and I tried not to think of Hazel's pink pussy flashing at me from that very spot.

The footage began on the exterior of the building with me and Hazel walking out of the club wearing wide smiles and loose legs.

"Guess we know why they were workin' so late," Slayer teased, and I flipped him off, my gaze never left the screen.

Fifteen minutes after we drove away, three men pulled in closer.

"Motherfuckers were already on the property."

That was a serious breach that we would have address.

"They were prepared," Holden said as we all watched them use crowbars and hammers to break out the windows, effectively bypassing the security alarm on the main entrance.

"Put automatic privacy blinds on the list for the remodel," Gunnar grunted in my direction, and I added it to my list.

Inside the club, the three men went absolutely fucking nuts, wrecking shit like they had a personal beef with us. But as one of the men drew closer, I recognized that familiar crop of blond hair.

"That's the guy from the bar, the younger one. Right?"

Gunnar gave a sharp nod. "That's him. It's all of 'em."

"We could just report them," Holden, the voice of reason inside the Reckless Bastards, said.

"No." Gunnar's tone was firm and ice cold. His gaze seared into Holden and then into me, Wheeler, Cruz and finally, Slayer.

"These motherfuckers violated our space. Our land. Our fucking club. That violation must be met with enough force to discourage any other fucking meathead from doing this dumb shit."

He punched his palm in the universal gesture of a man needing to kick the shit out of another man, face red as he looked at each of us again, daring us to downplay the fatal seriousness in his gaze.

"Fifty grand bonus check to the first Bastard to bring me one of these motherfuckers. Bring 'em to Hardtail. Quietly. Alive."

Without another word, Gunnar jogged down the stairs to stew in his anger alone, at least that was my guess.

Someone turned on some music and the rest of us got to work. The longer it took to get things right, the longer it would take the club to re-open which would fuck with our revenue. I couldn't let that happen on my watch, and I was already creating a mental list of tasks that needed to be done and vendors we needed to call. Immediately.

"Need an extra pair of hands?"

I didn't need to look up to know it was Mitch. The man seemed to be everywhere lately, or maybe I was just more aware of him since he held all my secrets. It was a hell of a thing to trust a man, hell *anyone*, so much, but Mitch wasn't all that bad. Though I'd never admit that to him.

"Hey Doc, grab a broom or a trash can and toss what looks like it belongs in the dump. Then you can tell me what you think this dream means about me and an old nurse with big ta-tas." Cruz could always be counted on for a laugh or two and today the MC needed as many as we could get.

Instead of going straight to Cruz, Mitch made a stop beside me.

"Joplin, how are you?" To most people it sounded like a benign question, but I knew better.

"Good, but now isn't exactly a good time to talk."

"I'm not trying to have a session," he whispered. "Just checking in." His searching eyes missed nothing and even though I knew it was pointless to hide it, I didn't want to get into it here. With all the guys around.

"You seem tense."

"Yeah, well you'd be fucking tense too if someone trashed a year of your life, Doc. I appreciate the concern, but now really isn't the fucking time for this."

"Maybe not," Mitch said, getting in my face for the first time. Mostly he was content to mentally poke at my wounds and scabs, but today he was feeling brave.

"But it'll be too fucking late if you're dead because your head isn't on straight." His chest heaved and his eyes were dark and angry. Real.

Shit, Mitch was right. I couldn't afford to put any of my brothers at risk, and I couldn't afford to not come back. There was so much to say to Hazel, first.

"Fine. Not here." I turned to Slayer and shrugged. "I'll be downstairs if you guys need anything."

"We're fine, bro. Go get your head on straight so we can kill some shit sacks."

Cruz clapped me on the back again and shoved us both towards the stairs. As I headed down the stairs, I heard Cruz's voice. "Cleaning always goes down a little easier with some tequila!" So apparently, the guys drank and partied while they cleaned.

And lucky fuck that I was, I got to talk about my goddamn feelings.

Chapter Twenty-Four

Hazel

"Mmm, now that's an alarm clock I can get down with."

I woke up stretching my aching muscles and arching my back, but that wasn't what woke me up, no. What woke me up was soft lips surrounded by raspy whiskers, brushing over my nipples.

"Good morning to me!" Saint's lips were soft and playful, something I wasn't used to in bed.

"What am I, chopped liver?" He looked up at me in the space between my tits, his eyes sparkling with heat and mischief.

"What's wrong with chopped liver? I think it gets a bad reputation when it's really not all that bad."

I laughed when Saint nipped at the side of my boob playfully.

"I'm serious."

A growl came from deep in his throat and hit me right between the thighs. "I've missed this body."

For a second, just a fraction of a second, I thought that sentence would end differently, which scared the shit out of me, and I turned into his embrace and pressed my lips to his, slowly. Sensually.

"My body missed you too, Saint. So. Fucking. Much."

Our early morning sex wasn't a soft and gentle affair, but it wasn't as hot and dirty as it had been the last time at the club. The forest room. Holy shit I would never look at the great outdoors the same again. But that was a thought for a different time because I had a hot as fuck, butt naked man brushing his lips all over my electrified skin.

We came together hot and hard and fast. It was dirty but not filthy, and very satisfying. I was pretty sure I'd be wearing a smile the whole day. There were no toys or tricks, no kink either. Just straight vanilla sex—in a bed. It was so intense that I knew I'd been lying to myself, wholly and completely, about my feelings for Saint.

Which meant I needed distance. A lot of fucking distance.

A solitary shower wasn't an option, not when Saint joined me just seconds after I got the water switched to the perfect temperature. How in the hell was I supposed to resist a hot naked man, with tattoos and muscles as far as the eye could see? And then when he looked at me so intensely, his eyes dark and sensual, all I felt was cared for. Cherished. Adored.

I wasn't supposed to be feeling shit like this. Not for Saint—or anyone else for that matter. Those kinds of feelings led to even messier things that I had no business thinking about, so I was happy when we were fully dressed, and Saint was all business.

"I won't be around today. The club still needs a fuck ton of work."

If I was a normal girl, I'd probably be thinking how convenient it was that he had a full day of work right after a long night of fucking. But I wasn't normal. And it didn't bother me.

Much.

"I could help if you guys need an extra pair of hands."

"No," he snapped. "It's too dangerous."

"Dangerous? Look, I'm not trying to get clingy or anything crazy like that. This is my job, too, and I kind of need it. So if helping clean the place up helps to get it back open sooner, then I'll do it."

"Is that fucking job all you care about?"

The anger in his words took me back a literal fucking step.

"Whoa. Seeing as it's how I'm able to take care of myself, yeah it is what I care about. I don't have a big family or any family really, never mind a fucking biker gang to help me out. So excuse me for thinking about myself."

He was an ass. All the other shit I thought I saw in him must have been sex goggles. Yeah, that was it. The dick was so good it had me seeing shit when there was nothing to see.

Saint got in my face, a dark scowl marring his handsome features. "Look around sweetheart, yes the fuck you do."

That sounded great in theory. Right now he might mean it, but in real life? No fucking way.

"I don't need you to pretend like you care, Saint. We both know you only asked me out so you could find out who was robbing the stores in town, which I admire. But you didn't have to lie about it."

And that was the part I couldn't easily forget. The lie, and how easily he'd done it. So effortlessly.

"I think we both know I would have fucked you anyway. In fact, I'm pretty sure I did."

He took a step forward, looking hurt when I took one away from him. It wasn't my intention to hurt him, but I needed to protect myself; when he was close, I couldn't think straight.

"It wasn't like that."

His words said it wasn't, but the guilt swimming in his eyes told me otherwise.

"I don't want to fight with you Hazel. I can't, not when I'm not sure if I'll even make it home tonight."

I wanted to be cynical and cold and unfeeling. I wanted to tell Saint that I didn't give a shit about his little biker gang mission, because for all his talk about me, that was all he cared about. But something in his tone gave me pause.

"What's that supposed to mean?"

I couldn't forget that, despite his quiet, nice guy persona, he was a skilled liar. A trained killer and now, a biker with a vendetta. There were more reasons *not* to trust him, than to trust him.

"Me and Slayer are going out tonight to find these assholes. We can't let what they did to The Barn Door go unpunished, and with their escalating crimes in town, we can't afford to let them get bolder. More confident."

He took a step back and started to pace the length of the room.

"We need to end this shit once and for all, Hazel. And I have to help."

Instantly, a feeling I'd only ever felt for Jessie and myself bubbled to the surface. Fear. Hard and pulsing and very fucking real fear for Saint pumped through my veins. I didn't need to close my eyes for the worst-case scenario to play out, because I'd been seeing it in my dreams almost nightly since I met him.

"You can't."

His lips twitched in amusement. "So you *do* care."

"I never said that, but I've been having...dreams. About you."

Why the fuck was this so hard to say? He was just a man, not even my man.

"Yeah? Well I've been having dreams about you too, sweetheart."

I rolled my eyes and folded my arms across my chest, glaring at him.

"That's not what I meant. My dreams aren't...sexual. At all. Your eyes were open and there was b-b-blood on your face and hands...it was...bad."

I shook my head to knock the images loose, unwilling to see them one more fucking time.

"Shit, Hazel. I'm gonna be fine. I swear."

I shook my head again, stepping away from his touch.

"You don't know that. I didn't know what they were at first, these dreams. I thought it was just my subconscious way of warning me off you from the beginning but now I see."

"I'll be fine," he insisted again, this time with a bit more certainty that did fuck all to sooth my worries. His hands dropped to my shoulders, rubbing soothing circles that made me want to lean into him, which was exactly why I leaned away.

Then again, it wasn't his job to soothe my worries. Just because I had gone all female and squishy with emotions I couldn't afford to have right now, didn't mean that Saint had too.

In order to separate my feelings from him, from this situation, I needed distance.

"You're right," I told him and took a few steps back under the guise of finding my shoes.

"You know better than I do what you can and can't handle."

It wasn't my business and it wasn't my concern.

"It's okay to be scared, Haze. I'm afraid too, but I have to do this."

Foolish male pride.

"I'm not telling you not to. Ignore me, that was a moment of bullshit. You do you."

His smile was almost sad as he leaned in and brushed a gentle kiss across my lips.

"I care about you, too, Hazel, and yeah, it scares the fuck out of me too."

Without another word, he walked out the front of the bunkhouse, leaving me with only the sound of my racing heart and his heavy footfalls across the wood until he reached dirt.

At least I wasn't alone in my feelings, but that wouldn't do shit for me if Saint didn't come back tonight. Maybe this was a sign that it was time to ditch Opey. It was time to move on before anyone caught a case of feelings—or worse—decided to act on them.

Chapter Twenty-Five

Saint

"I can't believe you brought Hazel here," Slayer said, disbelief shining in his eyes from only the lighting available in Rusted Roof's parking lot. "More than that, I can't fuckin' believe it worked."

That was a relative term and I snorted.

"I wouldn't go so far as to say all that. Besides, here is where we found those assholes."

And that was why we were back for more. It was a simple solution but one that had a good chance of working, which is why I was headed inside on my own. A deep breath rushed out of me, proving to us both that I was more nervous, more anxious than I led on.

"You ready man?"

Slayer's voice was calm, even and there was no judgment in his voice, though I wouldn't blame him if there was.

I nodded. "I'm ready."

"You sure? 'Cause if not, we can figure out a new plan. We can do this another time."

I wasn't sure about anything, then again, I figured that level of certainty was left in the desert. With the big guns.

"I'm determined to see this through, Slayer. I'm as ready as I can be. And if I need you, you'll come runnin'. Right?"

"As long as there's not a woman suckin' my dick, I'll always come runnin' man."

I laughed at his crazy ass words. "As long as you come running, I'm fine with it."

"I got a perfect view of the front entrance. You know the plan."

Yeah, I did. I stepped from the beat up old pickup truck, and repeated the steps in my mind, more as a way to keep me calm and focused than a way to remember. I stepped inside the bar, dark and dank, and ordered a beer while I did a rotation of the room.

The place was packed, thanks to a live performance from a local country band. That meant I had to carefully pick my way through line dancers, revelers, cowboys and even cowgirls on the prowl.

The place was dark and smoky since people could still smoke indoors in most places in Texas, and that made it harder to see. The music and nonstop chatter of customers trying to be heard *over* the music made it hard to focus on one thing, but I managed. The flashing lights, the loud noises were determined to make every step of this task as difficult as possible. But as soon as I spotted a familiar head of blond hair, I headed in that direction.

"Hey sugar, how's about a dance?"

A much too young redhead in painted on jeans and a red and white polka dot bra-like shirt, pressed up against me and flashed a dimpled smile.

"Maybe later? Right now I'm lookin' for someone."

"I'm right here, baby."

She cooed in an attempt to be sexy, to look sexy, but she failed miserably. That baby voice turned me off right along with her persistence.

"Not you." I grabbed her wrist and plucked it from my shoulder. "Excuse me."

"Jerk."

I gave her my back and headed in the direction of the young blond asshole, who I still owed a pounding for putting his hands on Hazel. Now I owed his ass a lot more than that. The redhead was the least of my worries and chances were good she'd already found another sucker to latch onto.

I settled at the left end of the bar so I could keep an eye on the asshole, who was playing pool with a new group of guys. Most of them I recognized as locals, ranchers enjoying a night out to break up the back-breaking monotony of ranching. Said asshole laughed and joked, seemed like a regular twenty-something instead of a fucking criminal who enjoyed taking shit from people he didn't earn.

Finally, the asshole spotted me. His initial response—fear—flashing hard in his baby blue eyes. His expression quickly turned into a smug smirk, but it was too late for false bravado, I'd already seen what was in his heart.

Fear.

And I would use it to fucking destroy him. I watched him, happy to play the role of jokester with the good time guys. I kept my eyes on him just long enough to make him uncomfortable, and without his bodyguards around, he was a scared little pussy. My gaze followed him wherever he went, making sure that motherfucker couldn't breathe without me knowing about it first.

Eventually, I made it to the bottom of the beer bottle and headed for the bathroom, which in a dive bar like this meant a room with one toilet and a filthy ass sink. *At least I can take a piss in peace.* It was a damn psychic thought 'cause when I stepped back out into the hall, the young punk was there, looking angry and ready to fight.

"I'm not afraid of you."

"Congratulations. But you should be."

He smirked and got in my face, thinking those few inches he had on me was supposed to scare me off. I pulled myself up to my full height, which was unnecessary because where the kid was long and lean, I was thick and solid muscle. Insomnia meant that I'd kept up with PT as good as any active servicemember.

"Yeah and why is that?"

"Because you and your friends made a grave mistake. You fucked with the wrong people and now you'll have to pay."

This hadn't been part of the plan but it was the perfect set up for the next part.

"Don't take my word for it, just watch and see."

I made my way through even more dancers and partiers gyrating to a country-rock version of some song that the whole damn bar seemed to know, and out into the night air.

I pulled one of Slayer's cigarettes from my pocket and lit it up, smiling when I realized that big crazy fucker had mixed half tobacco and half weed. One puff. Two puffs. On the third, the front door smacked open and blondie made his appearance.

"You can't fuckin' threaten me, you piece of shit. Don't you know who I am?"

"No," I told him between puffs. "And I don't really give a flying fuck either."

Another puff had me butting up against the filter and I flicked it onto the ground and walked away.

"Hey, fuck you, man!"

There was part of me that hoped the kid wouldn't do it, wouldn't try to gain an advantage by sucker punching me. I'd hoped that he wasn't that kind of man, but when one hand gripped my shoulder, those hopes were fucking dashed.

I spun around and released a lightning quick punch to his nose and then his gut. Blood instantly poured from his nose even as he doubled over in pain and choked on his effort to get oxygen into his lungs.

"Keep your fucking hands to yourself kid."

He stood wearing a bloody smile.

"Or what?"

He lunged at me, and I stepped to the side just in time for the dumb asshole to catch a pickup truck door right to the head.

"Ow, fuck!" He writhed, mostly in silence, while Slayer and I looked on, amused as shit.

"Or, you might find yourself in a position you couldn't possibly imagine."

He looked up at me and then Slayer, calculating just how much he'd fucked up by following me out of the bar, and then he groaned, "Fuck me."

"You're pretty kid, but you ain't my type."

Slayer laughed and dragged him by one leg around the back of the truck, lifting him easily into the cab with a loud thud.

"What the fuck, man?"

He sat up and looked around as the situation finally dawned on him, kicking at Slayer's attempt to grab his ankle. "Get the fuck away!"

Slayer laughed. "Now's not the time to act like a scared little virgin, boy. You're in the grown folks shit now."

When the kid wouldn't stop kicking, Slayer hopped into the cab in one fucking move. With both feet.

"You have two choices here, let me hook you up in here so you don't try to jump out."

"No thanks," the asshole kid spat like a petulant fucking child.

"Or you can jump out on the highway, and I'll just shoot you in the knee and put you back in here. Either way, you're ours. Got it?"

His eyes widened and the fear I'd seen earlier had returned.

"Got it," he said reluctantly and stuck one leg out.

Slayer shackled him to the bar that ran along one side of the cab, jumped down and hopped behind the steering wheel like this was everyday work for us.

I guessed, in a way, it was.

Chapter Twenty-Six

Hazel

"Holy shit, Haze. You have *feelings* for him."

Jessie whispered it like it was a bad word, the awe in her voice making me roll my eyes over the phone.

"Actual real feelings. I can hear it in your voice."

"Hate is a feeling. Lust is a feeling, Jess."

I didn't hate Saint even if I did resent these feelings that made me feel weak, vulnerable and out of sorts. I hated the uncertainty of feeling shit for another person, especially someone as secretive as Saint.

Jessie laughed. "If hate was all you were feeling, you wouldn't sound so tortured and confused."

Another strike against having someone who knew me so well.

"Fine, yes I like him. All right? He's nice and sexy, and he can be funny when he's not trying to be. But I don't trust those feelings. What if it's nothing more than the high of having good dick in my life again?"

I didn't think it was, but a girl could hope, right?

"Bull. Shit. If it was just the dick, you'd be fine right now, maybe craving another ride, but that's it. So what's the real problem?"

Jessie was my people, the only person I trusted with my secrets. "I don't trust him."

There, I said it. Saint seemed like a good guy but this whole biker club thing sounded like a life filled with trouble, and I'd already had more than my fair share of that. And I was pretty damn sure that I couldn't be with a man who didn't talk, didn't share, and didn't open up. Ever.

"Has he given you any reason not to trust him, or is this where you sabotage anything that resembles happiness?"

"I don't sabotage," I insisted but Jessie's laughter drowned out my weak ass protests. "Okay fine, maybe

I do but it's only because I can see trouble before it lands me in a pile of shit."

I didn't possess Jessie's ability to forget all the bad shit that had happened to us. It served as a constant reminder and any man I met who set off alarm bells got his walking papers.

"Sure. Maybe. But love is also about leaping, about taking the risk without knowing how it'll all end."

Her voice was that of a woman confident in the love she had, from her man and her family. I envied that confidence, but I also didn't trust it.

"I don't have to know how it'll end Jessie because I know it will end. Badly. Besides, I have no idea where he is or when he's coming back. Hell, he might not come back at all."

Whatever was happening tonight was dangerous, and Saint was willing to pay the price. And for what?

"He didn't come home at all last night, and I haven't heard a word at all today."

"The fact that you're worried means you care. If you're not gonna come to Oklahoma with us, stay in Texas and see where this thing with Saint is headed."

"Certain heartache," I told her honestly. "Anyway, enough of my stupid drama. What's up with you?"

"The same old…hang on."

The line went silent as Jessie dealt with another mom or farm emergency and when she came back, she was rushed. That meant the end of our conversation.

"Sorry Haze, a peanut butter artist has painted the kids all over and guess who has to clean it up?"

"Not me," I told her with a grateful laugh. "But photos will be greatly appreciated."

"Oh there will be plenty because I plan to post them around the house when the kids are teenagers. None of us will ever forget."

Another laugh escaped before we said our goodbyes and the quiet in the bunkhouse highlighted the differences in our lives.

Jessie's filled her life with people from her kids and her husband to ranch hands and neighbors while my life was solitary. Singular. Quiet. Not that I didn't love my life, it was just...*incomplete.*

Sometime later, I found myself standing on the freshly painted porch that led to the main house, where Gunnar lived with Peaches and Maisie. The little girl sat on the glider with her legs folded under her, a doll in a ball gown in one hand and a toy horse in another.

"Hey, Maisie."

She looked up with her adorable crooked smile and big blue eyes.

"Hi Hazel! My doll got a new dress!" She held up the green gown with a sweetheart neckline and a gorgeous train.

"It's beautiful. I wonder if it comes in my size."

She giggled and the sound made me smile, just as it did when Jessie's kids laughed and called me Aunt Hazel.

"You're too big. It's doll size."

"Story of my life, kid. Is she going to a party or riding a horse?"

Maisie looked at me like she was the adult, and I was the kid who'd just said something foolish.

"She's riding her horse to the party. Her party because she's the best at everything."

In that moment, I envied that doll who was badass enough to ride a horse in a ball gown, while I hemmed and hawed over my stupid feelings for Saint.

"Sounds pretty cool. Should you be out here alone?"

"No, she shouldn't."

Peaches stood between the screen door and the hall that led into the main house with her arms folded and an inscrutable expression on her face. She aimed it right at the adorable little girl who wasn't fazed at all.

"She's supposed to be on the couch with her dolls."

"This is a couch," she insisted with the gall of a child at least twice her age. "And my baby doll is right here!"

"Maisie," Peaches said, her voice firm and maternal, much like Jessie's.

The little girl let out a pouty sigh and slid down until her feet touched the ground. She grabbed her doll, and I said, "She's a handful," as I watched her scramble inside.

Peaches laughed. "She's stubborn just like her brother. It must be a family trait."

Her tone was a little grouchy but affectionate. I wondered what it would be like to have people who cared even when caring was difficult.

"What's up, Hazel?" she said, turning her big, luminous eyes on me once the screen door slammed behind Maisie.

I shrugged, unsure how to explain that I was bored and tired of the silence so I came in search of companionship.

"Nothing."

I could have asked about Saint, but I refused to go there. If Peaches knew, Gunnar had wanted her to know so she wouldn't worry, and I wasn't ready to hear that. Yet.

"What's going on?" Peaches blinked, her eyes shocked for just a second before she quickly covered it up. "Martha and her evil spawn are busy in the kitchen, cooking up some food to last for a few days."

On the surface it was a pretty harmless statement but given what little I knew of what was going on, I knew it was anything but.

"Gunnar's giving them a few days off."

More vague answers so I just nodded.

"Well I just stopped by to see what you were up to, but I think I'm gonna head into town. Maybe grab a bite to eat and check on my apartment."

If it hadn't been touched yet, I could stay there tonight and decide what to do next.

"I wouldn't do that if I were you."

Her tone changed, hardened and I didn't like it.

"Saint wants you here."

"When he's done with whatever secret society business he has, he can come find me for a fuck, Peaches. This isn't my home. It's my job."

"Bullshit."

I shrugged. "Think what you want, but it's the truth. Since you're busy, I guess I'll see you around."

"Wait." She let out a frustrated sigh and walked down the porch steps. "They found one of the guys last night, the ones responsible for the robberies and vandalism. He's somewhere on the property."

Peaches didn't want to share the information with me, but just as I suspected, Gunnar had told her the truth. So she wouldn't worry.

Because he cares. I folded my arms protectively at that thought and shook away the hurt and disappointment that tried to well up within me. *Nope, no thank you. No way.*

"All the more reason I shouldn't be here." Trouble would be headed this way and the last thing I wanted was to get caught up in the middle of it.

Especially since Saint didn't care enough to tell me the truth about what was happening. And that fucking hurt.

"Stay," she insisted. "His asshole friends will be pissed when they realize he's missing and they'll be out for revenge. If they spot you out there alone," she shrugged and snapped her fingers. "You'll be easy pickin's. Wouldn't want something to happen to you."

I barked out a laugh at that. "Yeah, I don't think anything's going to happen. I'll be fine."

"We can debate the truth of that later, but how about a little bit of common sense, first? You think they'll care *or* believe you when you say you don't belong to the MC? Because they won't, and they'll do what they want to you just to get to the club."

"I don't belong to the MC or anybody else."

"Argue with me all you want Hazel, just keep your ass on the property. I can't have Gunnar's mind conflicted because he's worried that Saint's head isn't in the game. They need to focus so they can end this shit, and we can all go back to our regularly scheduled lives."

Without another word, Peaches turned and stomped back up the steps. Pissed off at me.

Like any of this shit was my fault.

What*ever*. I didn't need them. I didn't need anyone.

KB Winters

Chapter Twenty-Seven

Saint

Blood. It was everywhere, staining my fingertips and knuckles red, clumped under a few nails too. It was the exact place I didn't want to ever be again. Not fucking ever. Blood on my hands, my shaking hands and not even another one of Slayer's fucking nicotine-weed sticks could stop the shaking.

I stood outside one of the many non-descript looking buildings on the Hardtail Ranch, one hand-rolled smoke between my fingers and the weight of the fucking world on my shoulders. I'd left the service after losing all my friends in one fucking firefight, but it was being a hired gun that really pissed me off.

"It's the same shit all over again."

Holden stood beside me as quiet and stoic as ever. His wide shoulders were as straight as his spine, thick hair immovable as he shook his head.

"That's bullshit and you know it. You had a choice, joining this MC, you had a fucking choice, to become one of us. And unlike the service, you can leave at any time."

He swung his dark eyes to mine, his gaze fierce like I'd struck a nerve.

But Holden was right, I did make a choice. A commitment. A promise. To this MC and to these men. I agreed to become a Reckless Bastard knowing what it meant and what was expected of me. Gunnar had laid it all out, clear as day. Weekly meetings. Don't share MC business with anyone. Ever. And never, ever, let a woman come before Reckless Bastards. And I agreed to become a brother. Willingly.

"You're right. Thanks Holden." Him being right didn't stop my fucked up mind from going to fucked up places, though. Pounding that kid, no matter how much that fucker deserved it, had me dealing with some shit that I didn't have the time for. Not right now.

"That doesn't make it any easier."

Holden nodded like he understood and I knew to a certain extent, he did. It wasn't the same. It never was the same for any of us, but that was a fact we all understood.

"No one said this would be easy. Protecting life never is and it shouldn't be. But these guys, Saint, they didn't fuck up a bunch of mailboxes. They put an old lady in the hospital. Those fuckers hurt people in our town. In MY goddamn town, man!"

Holden rarely got pissed, so I knew he was feeling it deep to react so strongly.

"They can't get away with it. They won't."

"Of course they won't, Mah-Dick."

He glared at the use of his nickname and that was enough to inject a bit of levity into the night.

"Just because it's hard and fucking my head up, doesn't mean I'm not on board. I am."

"Good. Because this is just the beginning, and we all need to keep our focus until they've been dealt with. For good."

Holden was right and logically, I knew it. Taking the blond asshole was step one. Step two had been to get him to talk, to tell us who ran their little band of criminals and find out why they were targeting Opey. But where the kid lacked sense, he made up for it with heart. So far we hadn't gotten shit out of him.

"Then I guess we'd better get back in there and find out who the fuck they are *before* they find out who *we* are."

When this MC business was done, I needed to go see my girl.

If she would have me.

And right now, that was a big fucking *if*.

Chapter Twenty-Eight

Hazel

The sound of the screen door that allowed the bunkhouse doors to remain open when the Texas heat became unbearable interrupted my packing. I rolled my eyes, knowing it was Peaches trying to change my mind. Again.

"Don't try to talk me out of this, Peaches." I went over my speech knowing what a hardass she could be when she wanted her way. "My mind is made up and I'm leaving. For good."

No, I wouldn't say that. She didn't need to know all my plans. This wasn't the first place where I packed up and got the fuck out of town without warning, and it wouldn't be last. It was why I packed light and why I went out of my way not to form connections.

The harder it was to say goodbye, the more pain I had to carry with me. No fucking thanks.

When Peaches didn't respond right away, something inside of me froze, went ice cold, and my hand wrapped around the first hard thing I could find, a jar of moisturizer.

"Nothing to say?" My voice was shaky but I got the words out.

But when the figure appeared, it wasn't Peaches. It was one of the guys from that bar Saint and I went to on our first date. *Only date. And it wasn't even a real date.*

"Oh, I've got plenty to say, sweetheart. Not sure you wanna hear any of it though."

Long brown stringy hair that was about three days past needing a wash hung around his shoulders and forehead, and he wore a wild look in his red-rimmed eyes. I knew that look well, one of hate and disdain, mixed with a sick desire. And some drugs. I'd seen it for the first time in my second foster home when my thirteen-year-old foster brother walked in on me undressing and couldn't look away from my skinny nine-year-old body. I saw it again on the face of my fifth foster dad when I turned fifteen.

I took a step back and the greasy asshole smiled.

"What I want is to know what the fuck you're doing in here?"

A deep laugh rumbled out of him. "I'm looking for your fuckin' boyfriend. He and his buddies have my brother, and I ain't leaving here until I get him."

The look in his eyes told me the one thing I already knew for certain; any harm that came to me would be a bonus for him.

I folded my arms. Scared shitless, but trying like hell to look unconcerned, I gave him a careless shrug.

"Nothing to do with me. I don't have a boyfriend, and I don't know anything about your brother. I don't even know who he is."

"Bullshit," he spat in my direction. "You're his bitch, which makes you perfect leverage. He gives me my brother back and his skanky piece of ass gets to live."

Fuck. My heart pounded, knowing there was no way out of this without someone getting hurt. It looked like the universe had decided that I would be that someone. I couldn't let Saint or any of the others come to harm on my account, I wasn't worth the trade. I scoffed in his face and a smile teased my lips.

"That's where you're wrong, idiot. I'm not even a piece of ass, nothing more than a stupid girl who spent one ill-advised night with her boss."

I ignored the pinch in my heart at those words because no matter what Saint or Jessie or anybody said, no matter what my foolish heart believed, it didn't matter.

"Bullshit. You said—"

I cut him off quickly. "Fucker. I know what I said. I told your grabby little brother the same thing I tell every motherfuckin' asshole who thinks he can get a fuckin' piece from me."

That little shit just hadn't taken it as well as most men did.

"I don't believe you."

To punctuate his words, he produced a gun and aimed it right at my chest. I wanted to throw up. A wobbly but undoubtedly evil grin spread across his face, as greasy as his hair.

"But if you're telling the truth then I guess you're gonna die for nothing."

This was not what I signed up for. I had to get out of here if I wanted to live. I smiled because I was too afraid to do anything else. My heart thumped, and my whole life flashed before my eyes. Fuck this shit.

"What the fuck is so funny?" His fear and his anger were palpable. And irrational, so I continued to smile. "Answer me, bitch."

Ah, bitch. The name men go to when they're not clever enough to come up with something better.

"What's funny? You are. Coming in here alone like some kind of captain save-a-ho. You think killing me is going to do anything but rain down a never-ending shit storm on top of you and whoever you're working for?

They'll kill you and your baby brother twice just for the shit you caused. And that's if your precious little brother even made it through the night."

Just then Jessie's words came back to me. *One of these days that smart ass mouth of yours is going to get you into deep shit.* I guessed this was one of those days, and the shit was of the deepest variety.

Maybe my words struck a chord because the fucker lunged at me, and I chucked the jar of moisturizer I'd gotten on sale at a drug store somewhere outside of Austin straight at his thick fucking skull.

"You bitch! I'll kill you," he said as it bounced off his forehead.

"I think we've already established that," I told him and took a step or two back. Just far enough to bend down and pull my switchblade from my boot. A girl never could be too careful and being a girl in the foster care system had made me *very* careful. And wary of men.

"You. Can't. Win." His breaths sawed in and out of his body and the hand not holding the gun rested over his right eye where the jar had split his skin.

We were both exhausted and unwilling to back down, me because to do so meant certain death. Maybe worse. Him because he thought I was the path to his brother and deep down he knew I wasn't.

"Neither can you. The way I figure it, we're both as good as dead. The only question is which of us will meet our maker first."

A wicked smile spread across his sweaty face, and he scraped a forearm over his forehead, still working hard to catch his breath.

"Killing you first will give me the element of surprise."

Then he lunged at me, and I took two big steps to the side, changing my grip on the blade in my hand so when he came at me again, the blade slid into his skin like a hot knife through butter.

"Fucking bitch, you stabbed me!"

Throughout my life I hadn't had many chances to use the knife because most men were smart enough to leave me alone. And those *not* smart enough valued their dicks more than their pride and the threat of violence was enough. Not for this asshole, though. He wanted me to make him hurt so he had an excuse to make me hurt. *Oh well, let's see what you got asshole.*

"No, this is a stab," I grunted and jabbed the knife deep into his side again before I twisted it and yanked it out. "Piece of shit!"

As unladylike as it was, I spit at that motherfucker as he fell and turned to leave, forgetting my bag.

"Not so fast you rotten cunt."

He hissed his words as one bloody hand wrapped around my ankle and sent me flying face first to the ground. He laughed, but I showed him, turning to introduce the bottom of my boot to his ugly fucking face.

"The only rotten cunt is the one you crawled out of!"

I tried to stand but he was stronger. I was more determined, pulling my body along with his toward the screen door. Toward help and if not help, escape.

Every step forward took the effort of ten steps and when the door was in sight, the weight grew heavier as he crawled up my body, slowing me down. When his body covered mine, his hot breath fanned against my neck and my ear.

"Where is my brother?"

"Hopefully burning in the same trash pit as the rest of your family tree."

Holy shit, Jessie was right. My mouth was going to get me killed. I struggled against his weight, but I stopped as soon as his cock started to harden against my ass.

Without a word he straightened up and sent an elbow crashing into my side. I bit back the scream as pain flowed through me.

"Where is he?" He demanded, flipping me over like I weighed nothing, glaring down at me like he would have no problem taking what he wanted before he took my life.

"Fuck. You." I spit out at him.

One fist dropped down on my stomach and then another and another until all I could do was cover what I could for protection.

"Tell me you fucking bitch, where is my brother?"

"Fuck." The word came out on a choked cough from all the punches, but I was as stubborn as this motherfucker. "You."

He hit me again and again, using his weight to keep me pinned to the floor, my hands stuck between my legs and his knees.

"You're gonna tell me and then I'm gonna kill you."

When he bitch slapped me, I spit blood up at him just to piss him off. But what he didn't know was that I still had my blade, and I flipped it using my fingertips until I had the handle between my thumb and forefinger, pushing it slowly into the back of his thigh. "Eat. Shit. Motherfucker."

"You fucking slut!"

The butt of the gun came crashing down on my cheek and a second later I felt warmth ooze down my face even as my hands reached up and scratched at his face and eyes. But the gun hurt like a son of a bitch, and my vision flickered like a TV on the fritz. I knew I was going to die.

KB Winters

Chapter Twenty-Nine

Saint

"Some fuckin' guy just hired us. Me, my brother Stan, and his friend Shawn. Said to stir up shit on some hole in the wall town called Opey down in Texas. That's what we did."

He spat out the words, heaving breaths in and out through a likely broken nose.

"We came here and kicked up shit just like he wanted, but that old lady fell on her own. We didn't have anything to do with that. She shouldn't have tried to be a fucking cowboy and stayed in her fucking room."

Oh blondie was mad, downright pissed after nearly twenty-four hours of getting his ass beat between interrogations.

Slayer stood in front of him, an imposing figure beside the young blond. He backhanded the kid. Hard.

"Maybe you shouldn't have broken into her shit. Asshole." He hit him again out of pure anger, and the chair slid back a few inches.

The sound of a phone ringing pierced the mostly dark, silent room. Everyone froze. Even the kid.

"Yeah?" Gunnar's gruff voice sounded, and I didn't know how I knew but my gut tensed as we waited to hear the news.

"Fuck." He ended the call and let his blue gaze fall on each of us for just a moment before he started to explain and issue orders.

"There's a breach on the property. Probably pretty boy's crew. We need to get to the main house and bunkhouse ASAP. Cruz, stay with the kid."

"Got it, Boss." Cruz gave a salute, and we took off running to the waiting four wheelers just outside the short, squat building.

"Are we really a MC if we're get around on ATVs?"

Wheeler flashed a wide, almost pretty smile and took off ahead of everyone. Crazy fucker.

No one bothered to answer but as the vehicles cut across the land, I could tell his words added just the right amount of lightheartedness this situation called for. My thoughts, inevitably, drifted towards Hazel and the casual words I'd given her before leaving on MC business. I didn't want those words to be the last I ever said to her, those lukewarm emotions I let her believe was all I felt for her. *I care for you.* Those words seemed so fucking inappropriate now, when she was possibly facing down a very pissed off criminal.

When this was all over, I would take her for a long drive and tell her everything. I would tell her the truth about the men in my unit, the truth about the depth of my feelings for her, which only became apparent now. When I could lose her.

All the vehicles came to a stop in the space between the bunkhouse and the main house. My feet itched to head straight for Hazel. Gunnar saw me and nodded.

"Go. Slayer and Holden go with him. Wheeler, you're with me."

"What about me, Boss?" Ford stood by an ATV, his baby face scrunched in confusion, but the kid was eager to help.

Gunnar looked like he hadn't realized the kid was there.

"Come with me. We gotta find Peaches and Maisie first."

Before he was finished with his sentence, Gunnar was on the move, eating up the distance between him and his family, climbing the steps three at a time.

My feet pounded the dirt and gravel mixture until I yanked the screen door hard enough to pull it off the hinges. I ran inside like the devil was on my heels, going to the right side where Hazel kept her things and hoping like hell she was there with Gunnar's girls or, worse, had left my sorry ass hours ago. As long as she was safe, things would be...*shit*. She wasn't safe.

Too late, the details in the room hit me. The room was fucked up, evidence of a violent struggle everywhere but nothing hit me more than the sight I took in now. One of blondie's men straddling Hazel's hips as his fists rained down on top of her. I stood there, frozen. Unable to do a goddamn thing to save her, to help her. Nothing except look on like a frightened little cub waiting for his nuts to drop.

"What the—?" Slayer slammed into my back and pushed me aside, taking in the room in half the time I did. Only Slayer was a man of action and pulled out his weapon.

"Watch out for Hazel."

The words came out barely above a whisper, and I wasn't even sure if he heard me over the commotion, but Slayer took aim and the sound of a gunshot tore through the air followed by the grunt and thump of that asshole falling over. Onto Hazel.

My heart skidded to a complete stop as silence swirled around us. One shot. Followed by...nothing. There were no tearful screams from Hazel, no signs of relief at how close she'd come to dying, which left just one terrible, unthinkable conclusion.

Hazel wasn't relieved because she was the way she always was in my dreams. *Dead*.

"She's fine," Holden grunted as he tore the dark-haired man off Hazel, giving me a clear glimpse of Hazel for the first time.

She wasn't fine. The first thing I saw was her eye, swollen and purple, almost totally closed. But Holden was right. The closer I looked, I could see signs of life. The slow rise and fall of her chest, the color in her cheeks despite being unconscious.

Blood rushed through my head, pounding, as memories took over. Memories of the worst fucking day of my life when I lost my men. Blood soaked hands, familiar faces choking on lasts breaths, and dying smiles meant to soothe the living me. Except Hazel wasn't smiling or choking, she wasn't doing anything because she was out of it. Completely fucking unconscious. But Holden signaled he'd found her pulse.

"Thank fuck. We need an ambulance," I shouted to no one in particular as two pairs of strong hands lifted me up and pulled me away from Hazel.

"Come on, man."

Holden's deep southern drawl was soothing but nothing could help me, not with Hazel lying on the floor lifeless. Okay, not lifeless but my crazy heart and my fucked up mind didn't know the difference.

"No! She needs some help. Get her some fucking help!"

"We are," Holden whispered. "Doc is on her way. She'll check out Hazel and get her all fixed up. In the meantime, you need to calm down and get cleaned up."

"I don't give a shit what I look like." Slayer backhanded me and the fucker didn't even look apologetic. "Hey, what the fuck man?"

"You were spiraling. Clean yourself up because the last thing she needs to see when she wakes up is you, covered in blood and looking like a goddamn maniac."

He was right. I didn't like it, not at all, but Slayer was right. Resigned, I let them lead me away but my eyes never left Hazel, not until I could no longer see her. Only then did I let my body, my mind and my heart succumb to the memories.

Chapter Thirty

Hazel

"Good. You're finally awake."

A pretty brunette was looking down at me with a gentle smile and kind eyes.

"Where am I?"

"In the bedroom of the house. Glad you're talking. You had everyone worried."

I arched a brow. "Including you?" Whose house?

Her laugh was as pretty and feminine as she was. I wondered if she was one of those women who were always perfectly put together and wore a smile whether she meant it or not.

"Nah, I'm a doctor so I knew you'd be fine. Everyone else, though, wasn't so sure."

She struck her hand out so it was inches from mine. "Dr. Annabelle Keyes at your service, but you can call me Annabelle."

I accepted her hand and gave it a shake, wincing as pain tore through my midsection and my head.

"Hazel. Nice to meetcha, Doc. How am I?" I remembered the greasy brown-haired dude and fighting him in the bunkhouse, but after the gun hit my cheek everything got a little fuzzy.

Annabelle wore a sad smile as she took in my face, and I knew he must have fucked me up good.

"You're doing okay, considering the beating you took. A few bruises and abrasions so you'll be in pain for some time, but everything will heal good as new."

Everything except my mind. My heart. "What about the other guy?" Why wasn't I in a hospital?

Annabelle shrugged and turned away, trying very hard to appear casual.

"Not much I can do about a bullet to the chest."

She turned to me with a weak smile, and I decided question time was over.

"I'll give you enough pain killers for five days and I want you to get plenty of rest during that time."

Rest wasn't possible, not when I needed to work in order to have a place to lie down while I healed. Bills needed to be paid, including medical bills.

"Thanks, Annabelle. How much do I owe?"

She waved off the question. "It's been taken care of," she said vaguely.

"I didn't know doctors made house calls. Not even in Texas."

She didn't answer, but I was grateful that I wouldn't have to deal with law enforcement. "How long have I been out of it?"

"On and off for two days. I kept you sedated for the first day so I could monitor any swelling inside your head."

"Thanks for everything, Annabelle." Two days? I'd been lying in this makeshift hospital bed for two days? Alone?

"I'll come back to see you in a few days. Make sure you take it easy, Hazel." With a friendly wave, she left me alone with my thoughts, which inevitably turned to Saint.

Dr. Anabelle said house, but I think she meant bunkhouse. Saint lived in the fucking bunkhouse but even hours later, after the sun had set, no one came in except Peaches and Maisie for a visit. I was awake most of the time, now, and alert when Slayer stopped in to make inappropriate comments that made me smile. But Saint...well Saint was no fucking where to be found.

So much for caring about me, even as an employee or a friend, or just a fucking human being. Saint wasn't here, and he hadn't sent me any messages that said he wanted me to stick around or that he was even glad I'd survived the attack.

As Jessie would say, that in itself was a message. Instantly I knew what I had to do.

Leave Opey behind for good.

WICKED

***

I gave my apartment one last glance with a smile that I didn't really feel. I laid my head here at night, occasionally cooked meals, and showered here, but I hadn't done a thing to make this space feel like home. As I stood in front of the open duffel bag on my bed, I was happy I hadn't gotten too invested in this place, since I'd already given my landlord thirty days notice.

He wasn't thrilled, but after everything that happened with Edna Mae, he also didn't fight me. Which meant there was nothing tying me to Opey any longer. It was time to go.

Time to move on. Start over new someplace else.

Moving on meant I would miss my appointment with Annabelle in two days, but other than a little soreness in my midsection, I felt fine. Most of me felt fine anyway. Soon enough, the parts that felt less than fine would go back to normal, and this past year would be nothing but a memory.

A blip on the radar just like Denver and Chicago, San Francisco, Seattle, and Boston. Just another place I lived once.

My bags, all two of them, were packed.

A knock sounded on the door and for a moment, I froze. I didn't know what happened to the dead guy's brother, and I didn't care. Unless he was him on the other side of the door, ready to exact a little revenge. Slowly I walked to the door and lifted a shaky hand to use the door as leverage, letting out a sigh of relief at the unexpected sight of Saint.

He was the last person I expected to see since I hadn't seen him at all since he left my bed to go pick up that kid. By my count, that was at least five days ago. Maybe six.

"Saint. What are you doing here?"

He looked good, a little disheveled with his hair sticking up in all directions, and his t-shirt and jeans slightly wrinkled.

"What am I doing here? You left the ranch!"

"You're upset. Don't be. I'm fine. See?" I motioned to my body, biting back another grunt of pain, so he could see for himself that I was fine.

"You're not *fine,* Hazel."

"I *am* fine, Saint, and please do me a favor and don't act like you give a damn. This is the first time I've seen you in almost a week. A fucking week so don't show up on my doorstep acting like you have a right to question me."

Hurt flashed in his eyes, but I wasn't moved because I was hurt, too. Dammit.

"I'm sorry Hazel. So fucking sorry."

"Save it for someone else."

I wasn't in the mood to hear his excuses and what was more, I was terrified I might actually believe him.

"I froze, Hazel. I saw you lying there with that motherfucker on top of you and instead of rushing to your aid and pounding the shit out of him, I fucking froze."

He raked a trembling hand through his hair and a frustrated breath rushed out of him, which yeah, went a long way in making me see just how tortured he was by what had gone down. Still.

"I had to get my head on straight before I could see you again because I was worried I'd lose my shit."

He smiled but there was no humor in it. "I lost my shit anyway, but I'm good. Mitch is a good head shrinker, and I'm healed up enough to say what I need to say."

That was good news. I knew there was something dark and troubling within him, but he never shared and I never insisted, mostly because it wasn't my place.

"Good for you, Saint. That's good news."

I could see the difference in the way he carried himself, the half-smile that slashed across his face and the lightness that floated off his broad shoulders. I was happy for him, truly I was, but this wasn't about me. Not really. My bag waited on the bed, and I went back to it, shoulders squared with determination.

WICKED

"Stay, Hazel."

"I can't."

There was nothing to stay for, certainly not a man who hadn't checked on me at all in five days.

"You can. I know you can."

I shouldn't have looked at him, dammit. I knew it was a mistake because that soft smile he wore went a long way to softening my resolve. To making me want to hear what he had to say next. Even though I shouldn't.

"I care about you, Hazel."

I had to snort a laugh at that. It was rich, coming from him.

"Have I given you any indication that I need you to lie to me about your feelings? Ever?"

Care. It was such a bullshit word that meant nothing. Hell, I cared about Edna Mae and every other person kind enough to smile at me on the street, but would I trust them with my life? Fuck no, I wouldn't.

"We're both fucked up but in different ways. I know that and I don't give a shit. I love you, Hazel, and I want us to be fucked up together."

His grin squeezed at my heart and brought a smile to my face.

"I love your sassy fucking mouth. Your don't fuck with me attitude that seems to come off you like smoke. Hell, I even love your kink."

He stepped closer and put a hand on my shoulder, resting it gently there as his thumb grazed my collarbone.

"I want to be better for you. For us. For the life we could have together."

If we were strong enough to go after it. Saint didn't say it, but he didn't need to.

"With you in a biker gang and me bartending at a sex club? That doesn't sound like the life I envisioned for myself."

He shrugged and flashed a playful, handsome smile.

"It'll be non-traditional, that's for sure. I just didn't peg you for a traditionalist. And it's a motorcycle *club,* not a gang."

His playful smile only grew and I felt my resolve weakening.

"Is your club as secretive as a gang? Not that I'm considering this, I just want the details." His lips twitched at the lie we both knew those words to be.

"There will be things I can't tell you, yeah. But I will always make sure you're safe. Protected. All of us will, Hazel. That's the deal. And we'll make a fuck ton of money."

I wanted to believe him, but there was too much evidence to the contrary. "What happened to the guy who attacked me?"

"Dead. Slayer put a bullet in him when I couldn't. Gunnar was pissed, but it's done."

A fact that still tortured him, despite all the head shrinking Mitch had apparently done. At least pissing the boss off still got a smile out of him.

My head began to nod absently. "What about the guy you went after, what happened to him?"

Saint sighed. "He's not dead, I know that much. Gunnar let him go with a message," he said, hesitation making his voice quiver.

"You think it's a bad idea?"

He nodded. "I think it's gonna come back to bite us all in the ass before we kill it."

Honesty. Even when I didn't want the gory details, it was always more refreshing than a pretty little lie.

"What did you do with the body?"

His lips twitched, and his brows rose. "You really want to know?"

Some things were best kept secret so I shook my head and grinned. "No. But, thank you for answering."

"So what do you say? Stay?" he pleaded.

"I'm not sure, but for you, Saint, I might be willing to try the biggest kink of all."

"And what's that?" he asked, a cheesy grin on his face.

"Normal." It was something I wished for as a kid and teenager in foster care, but as an adult I knew the dirty little secret.

Normal was overrated. Normal was miserable because people spent all of their time just trying to *be* normal.

Saint's face lit up with happiness, his dark features no longer brooding just darkly handsome as he gathered me in his arms and kissed me until I was breathless and clawing at his clothes, desperate to get him naked.

"Normal is boring, babe. Come back to the bunkhouse with me, and I'll build us our very own place." He leaned in and pressed a kiss to my jaw. "With our very own playroom."

My eyes closed at the promise in his tone. God I wanted that kind of normal. *My* kind of normal, where

I wouldn't constantly have to justify my issues, or explain them. Apologize for them.

"Are you sure, Saint? I mean, I know you only asked me out bec—"

He cut me off. "I asked you out *when* I did because it gave me the perfect excuse to ask you out. But that's all it was. An excuse. Do you need me to show you?"

Saint ground his hips against me, sensual intent burning deep in his eyes.

"Yes, please." It came out on a low moan, and before I registered what he was doing, Saint took his sweet ass time undressing me. Stripping me of every stitch of clothing I wore until I trembled with desire and shook in his arms.

"But first," he said with a sly smile and sat down on the bed, patting his lap. "We need to punish you for running off before we could talk."

"Punish?" I meant to sound outraged but the words came out on a breathy moan because the idea of

Saint doling out a little punishment had my panties good and wet. Soaked, in fact.

He nodded. Slowly. Licking his lips like I was the perfect snack. "A spanking is in order, I believe."

Fuck. Yes. Please. "Make it good, in that case."

"I plan to. And then I'm gonna fuck you hard and fast. Then slow and sweet. Kinky as hell and then so fucking tender it'll bring tears to your eyes. I'll make you come so hard you'll come again. And again. I'll keep making you come until you tell me you love me too, Hazel. Because I know that you do."

He was right. I could deny it all I wanted to, but love was the only fucking thing that made sense. Why everything felt so different with him, even sex. Especially sex. Why I was so drawn to him unlike any other man I'd ever met. Why I was ready to leave town and a good paying job just to get away from him. But love was scary shit and I was, let's face it, a big ol' scaredy cat.

"And then?"

A slow grin that matched my own spread across his gorgeous face. "And then I'll tell you that I love you too before I make you come. Again."

I trembled at his words, at the way his lips skidded down my overheated skin, at the feelings that welled up in my chest with every sweep of his hand, every glide of his tongue. But what Saint proposed, a twisted kind of forever with someone as fucked up as me? Well, how in the fuck did I say no to that kind of happy ending?

I didn't. "Then let's get back to Hardtail so you can show me just how much I love you, Saint."

We made it in ten minutes flat and by minute twelve I was hot, slick and wrapped around his cock like I was meant to be there.

By the third hour and countless orgasms, I was pretty sure that all the shit in my life had led me to Hardtail Ranch, to The Barn Door and the Reckless Bastards.

To Saint. He was mine. My forever. My reward.

Mine.

WICKED

And I wasn't letting him go.

Not ever.

* * * *

THE END

Acknowledgements

Thank you so much for making my books a success! I appreciate all of you! Thanks to all of my beta readers, street teamers, ARC readers and Facebook fans. Y'all are THE BEST!

And a huge very special thanks to Jessie! I'm such a *hot mess, but without your keen sense of organization and skills, I'd be a burny fiery inferno of hot mess!! Thank you!

And a very special thanks to my editors (who sometimes have to work all through the night! *See HOT MESS above!) Thank you for making my words make sense.

Copyright © 2019 KB Winters and BookBoyfriends Publishing LLC

KB Winters

About The Author

KB Winters is a Wall Street Journal and USA Today Bestselling Author of steamy hot books about Bikers, Billionaires, Bad Boys and Badass Military Men. Just the way you like them. She has an addiction to caffeine, tattoos and hard-bodied alpha males. The men in her books are very sexy, protective and sometimes bossy, her ladies are…well…*bossier*!

Living in sunny Southern California, with her five kids and three fur babies, this embarrassingly hopeless romantic writes every chance she gets!

You can reach me at Facebook.com/kbwintersauthor and at kbwintersauthor@gmail.com

Copyright © 2019 KB Winters and BookBoyfriends Publishing LLC

Printed in Great Britain
by Amazon